## "You're angry, aren't you, Blake?"

"I'm not sure angry begins to cut it." He paused to take a calming breath. He needed to concentrate to keep his cool. "Serena, I happen to be allergic to bee stings. The same kind of allergy that Nate has. The kind that I told you is commonly inherited."

"I didn't know about your allergy."

"You had no reason to. The subject never came up in the time we knew each other. But that's not the point," he said impatiently. "Even if the bee sting allergy had never come up, I could see right off that Nate may have inherited his good looks from you, but he never got that square chin or the shape of his head from you."

"No, he definitely didn't," she agreed softly.

"He's my son, isn't he?"

One word. "Yes."

# MONTANA MAVERICKS: WED IN WHITEHORN
## Brand-new stories beneath the Big Sky!

# MONTANA MAVERICKS

**JENNIFER GREENE**

lives near Lake Michigan with her husband and two children. Before writing full-time, she worked as a teacher and a personnel manager. Michigan State University honored her as an "outstanding woman graduate" for her work with women on campus.

Ms. Greene has written more than fifty category romances, for which she has won numerous awards, including three RITA Awards from the Romance Writers of America in the Best Short Contemporary Books category, and a Career Achievement award from *Romantic Times Magazine.* She has recently been inducted into the Romance Writers of America Hall of Fame.

# MONTANA MAVERICKS

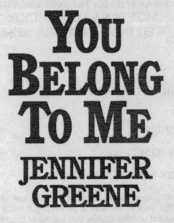

# YOU BELONG TO ME

## JENNIFER GREENE

Silhouette Books

Published by Silhouette Books
**America's Publisher of Contemporary Romance**

Special thanks and acknowledgment are given to Jennifer Greene for her contribution to the MONTANA MAVERICKS: WED IN WHITEHORN series.

 SILHOUETTE BOOKS

ISBN 0-373-65048-5

YOU BELONG TO ME

# MONTANA MAVERICKS

## Wed in Whitehorn

*Welcome to Whitehorn, Montana—
a place of passion and adventure.
Seems this charming little town has some
Big Sky secrets. And everybody's talking about...*

**Blake Remmington:** Trent's twin thought the revelation of their Kincaid roots would be the biggest shock in his life. Then old friend Serena Dovesong entered his examining room with her son in tow and he detected another secret in little boy Dovesong's eyes....

**Serena Dovesong:** A long-ago night of comfort had given Serena a precious memory...and her precious son, Nate. But she'd refused to "trap" Blake, instead freeing him to marry another woman and accept a coveted residency. She still feared Blake's attentions were inspired by duty, but could the look in *his* eyes possibly be...love?

**Homer Gilmore:** Lovably kooky Homer has seen an "alien" again—this one being particularly fond of the old Baxter land....

**Christina Montgomery:** Everyone's abuzz about the disappearance of pregnant Christina—psychic Winona Cobbs believes something bad's about to break in Whitehorn...again.

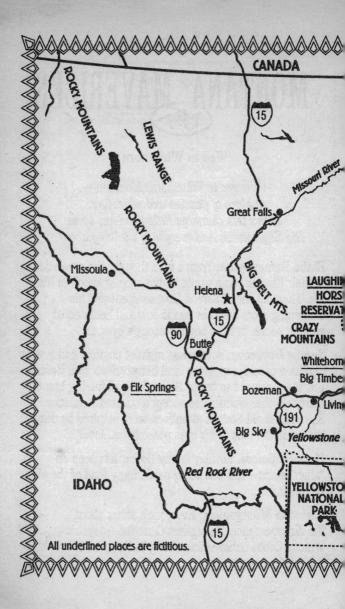

CANADA

ROCKY MOUNTAINS

LEWIS RANGE

ROCKY MOUNTAINS

Missouri River

Great Falls

Missoula

Helena

BIG BELT MTS.

LAUGHIN
HORS
RESERVAT

CRAZY
MOUNTAINS

Butte

Whitehor
Big Timber

Elk Springs

Bozeman

Livin

ROCKY MOUNTAINS

Big Sky

Yellowstone

Red Rock River

IDAHO

YELLOWSTO
NATIONAL
PARK

All underlined places are fictitious.

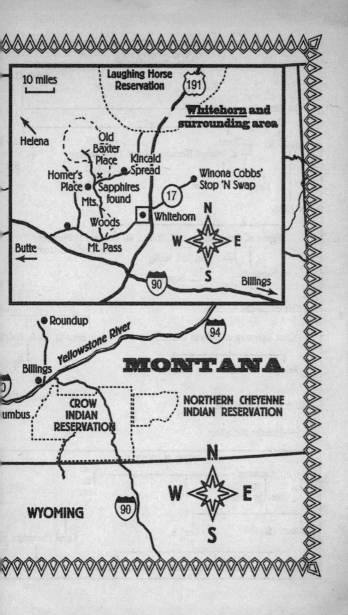

10 miles

Laughing Horse Reservation

191

**Whitehorn and surrounding area**

Helena

Old Baxter Place

Kincaid Spread

Homer's Place

Sapphires found

Winona Cobbs' Stop 'N Swap

17

Mts.

Woods

Whitehorn

N
W E
S

Butte

Mt. Pass

90

Billings

Roundup

Yellowstone River

94

Billings

**MONTANA**

Columbus

CROW INDIAN RESERVATION

NORTHERN CHEYENNE INDIAN RESERVATION

N
W E
S

WYOMING

90

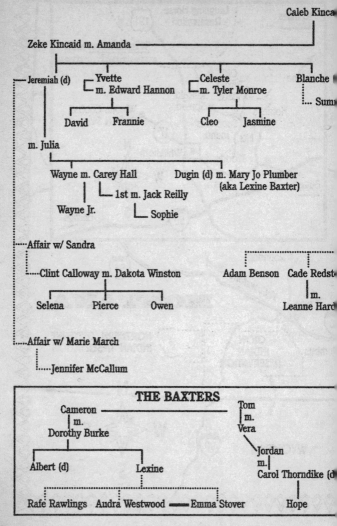

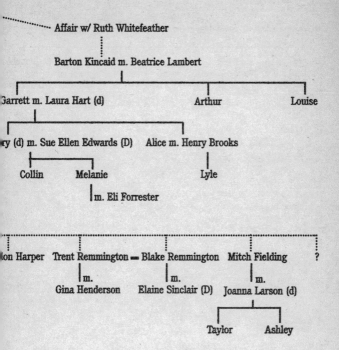

Affair w/ Ruth Whitefeather

Barton Kincaid m. Beatrice Lambert

Garrett m. Laura Hart (d)　　　　Arthur　　　　Louise

ry (d) m. Sue Ellen Edwards (D)　　Alice m. Henry Brooks

Collin　　　Melanie　　　　　Lyle

　　　m. Eli Forrester

lon Harper　　Trent Remmington ━ Blake Remmington　Mitch Fielding　　?

　　　　m.　　　　　　m.　　　　　　m.
　　Gina Henderson　Elaine Sinclair (D)　Joanna Larson (d)

　　　　　　　　　　　　　　Taylor　　　Ashley

Symbols
..... Child of an Affair
━ Twins
d Deceased
D Divorced

# One

"**Y**ou're going to be okay, Nate. I know you're feeling bad, but Dr. Carey will know just what to do." Serena Dovesong slammed on the brakes, yanked open the driver's door of her rusty red pickup and hurled around the front of the truck to the passenger's side. At rocket speed, she had her hands on her son.

"No, no, don't try to move on your own, sweetie. Just let Mommy carry you. A couple more minutes and we'll be inside the doctor's office. Everything's going to be just fine." Her heart was thumping to a frantic drumbeat, but she kept her voice as soothing as a love song. "Nothing to be scared of, lovebug. Nothing at all. Just hold on to Mom."

She was aware of leaving the keys and her purse in the truck, but carrying Nate was all she could handle. Besides, it wasn't as if she cared whether anyone stole the stuff. They could have it. They could have her truck, her money, and anything she owned—as long as her son was all right. And man, it had been a long time since she'd had to physically carry her six-year-old. He was heavier than a mountain. Please, God. Please...

The instant she charged onto Willow Brook Road, a car horn furiously blared, nearly scaring the wits out of her. She hadn't looked. Not just because she was so worried about Nate that she couldn't think, but because there was no reason to expect traffic— not on a blistering hot August afternoon in the quiet Montana town of Whitehorn.

The car swerved and Serena kept running, her arms cradling her son, sweat beading on her forehead and every place her baby's body touched hers. She always stayed cool in a crisis. Always. But damn. Nate's skin was clammy and he was limp in her arms. The darn kid should have been giving her a hard time about being carried like a baby. He should have been galloping around the street, giggling at the top of his lungs. He should have been noisy and mischievous and by this time in the day, she should have been cleaning up at least one scrape or cut, because Nate was an exuberant life lover and never had been afraid of a damn thing.

Nor was his mom.

Usually.

Serena gave herself credit for having an unusual amount of courage. But not where her son was concerned. The thought of anything happening to Nate drowned her heartbeat in a river of fear.

The sun fried through her dark hair, burned through her sandals. It had to be a hundred and ten, and the big sky looked bleached out and cloudless, not even a mist cloaking the Crazy Mountains to the west. And then, blessedly, there was sudden cool shade as she used her hip to push open the door to Dr. Carey Kincaid's office. Instantly she smelled antiseptic and alcohol, saw the usual lineup of miniature bodies in the pediatrician's waiting room, but the sights and sounds passed by in a blur.

"Serena? And Nate? What's wrong?" The buxom receptionist jumped up from her chair when she saw Serena hurtling past with Nate in her arms.

This was no hoity-toity big-city medical facility where anyone had to worry about formal rules. There were no strangers in Whitehorn. No one was going to misunderstand if she charged into the inside examining rooms without an appointment. "I need Dr. Carey! Right now! I almost headed for the emergency room, but her office was closer. This won't wait. Nate got stung by a bee. I know that sounds like nothing, but something's wrong. The stinger's out, and I put an ice pack on it, did all the obvious first-aid things—"

"Dr. Carey's not here today," the receptionist said, unrattled. "But you should have gotten the letter about her expanding the practice to include Dr. Remmington. In fact, he just started with us last week—"

"—but Nate broke out in this clammy sweat. And he started acting really dizzy, breathing in this strange way. It was just a bee sting! Only, in a matter of minutes, he suddenly seemed so sick, so I just grabbed him and drove here. I—" Serena suddenly stopped. "Did you say 'Remmington?'"

"That's right. Blake Remmington. The kids have been calling him Dr. Blake. Head into the third room on the right, it's free, and I'll go run and get the doctor."

"Hurry."

Serena heard the frantic note creep into her voice and purposefully lowered her tone—just as she purposefully banished any emotional response to hearing Blake's name. She could easily have ignored an earthquake right then. Nothing mattered but her son. Nothing. She forced a reassuring smile for Nate as she laid him on the white-papered examining table. "Hey, shortstop. You're looking better already." He was looking worse, his beautiful golden skin now a strange, alien gray.

"I want to go home, Mom."

"And we will. In just a little bit."

"My arm hurts."

"I'll bet it does." When she lifted the ice pack, her eyes stung with fear. The welt was still swelling. Bracing Nate with one hand—she was afraid he was dizzy enough to fall—she flicked on the cold faucet at the sink with the other and grabbed paper towels.

"I don't want to see the doctor. I don't want any shots. I just want to go home, Mom."

"Hey, me, too." She combed her fingers through her son's thick, straight black hair and pressed her lips against his flushed forehead, even as she was pressing the wet towels on the bee sting welt. "You know what? I'm rethinking that computer game you wanted."

"Wild Warriors?"

"Yeah, that one." The game that bugged her because it played up all the Native American stereotypes. The one she swore she'd never get him no matter how much he argued. But that was yesterday. "I'm thinking that you've been such a good squirt lately that you deserve a present."

"You said it was a dumb game. You said I was spending too much time on the computer." But hope was starting to shine in his eyes—enough hope to make him forget his hurt arm, at least for a second.

"I do think the game is dumb," Serena replied. "And I also think you're spending way too much time on the computer. But if you really want this Wild Warriors, what the hey." She wanted to buy him the game. And everything else he'd ever wanted. Anything to make him feel better. Anything. If Nate asked her at that second for the moon and the stars, she'd have sold her soul to try to obtain those for him, too.

"Mom. I'm not crying, because I'm too brave to cry. But I'm thinking about it. I'm thinking about it hard. My arm hurts. It really, really hurts. I am not having fun and I want to go home—"

From just behind her Serena heard the familiar masculine bass voice, rolling out like a sax playing slow, lazy blues.

"I'm Dr. Blake, Nate. And I can see right away what a brave, strong boy you are. But let's see if we can make you feel better so you won't have to try so hard.'' Blake Remmington stepped calmly into the room, his eyes fixed on Nate. "Did your mom have the chance to tell you that we're old friends? I always did think she was one of the most special people on the planet. I'll bet you think that, too, huh? Wow, that's quite a bump. I'm thinking you must have tangled with a bee the size of the Crazy Mountains. And I want you to tell me about it, but not yet. Right now I want you to be real quiet, and just breathe in and out for me, okay? Slow. Real easy. I can't hear anything else when I have the stethoscope in my ears, but after I listen to your heart, then you can talk all you want.''

Serena remembered the last time she'd seen a magician work his magic. Blake wasn't that different. He'd started talking from the minute he'd walked in, but it wasn't idle or gregarious chitchat. Instead he was using that easy, mesmerizing voice of his to soothe his young patient—and it worked. Nate fell silent as the doctor pressed the stethoscope disc on his chest and back. Blake's attention was focused completely on her son. And so was Serena's.

Still she felt Blake's swift glance at her, the way he inhaled her in a single gulp…and heaven knew, she was just as aware of him. Her nerves vibrated like a tuning fork identifying an old, familiar chord.

The years had changed him, but not much.

Not enough.

He wore no lab coat, just a blue T-shirt over chinos—casual, comfortable clothes that couldn't possibly intimidate a child. But the shirt was tucked in, the chinos belted, the city haircut conservative. Even in college, Blake had always colored between the lines—not because he was a follower in any way, but because he seemed to have been born with an old-fashioned sense of honor. Blake Remmington had always been the kind of man who said the right thing and did the right thing, no matter what the cost to himself.

Even barefoot, she knew he was an easy six-two, with the lean, lithe build of an athlete. He had no waist, no butt, but both his arms and shoulders were corded with muscles that stretched the seams of his shirt. He wasn't a muscle man, just physical by nature. Though his body hadn't softened in the last seven years, Serena sensed a hidden softness in him, just as she had back then.

His hair was a rich, dark brown; his skin ruddy. His eyes, a nonstop source of fascination for her—or they used to be. His eyes weren't just blue. They were compelling, sexy, changeable, sometimes the cold blue of an icy glacier, sometimes the hot blue of a raging fire. Whether they were cold or warm depended on whether you'd done something to tick him off or were a lover in his bed.

Nothing could be hotter than Blake's blue eyes— Serena knew that personally—but he never willingly let down his hair, even when the lights went off. He valued control, particularly in himself. The only time he openly revealed the soft side of himself was when he was around children. She hadn't known he'd become a pediatrician, but she remembered how he was around kids even as a med student. A child looked at him and instantly trusted. Somehow kids sensed his gentleness, his integrity. Maybe they even intuited that this was a man who could loudly lose his temper, yet never would with a child. That was an absolute. There were a lot of things that used to be absolutes with Blake Remmington.

Her palms suddenly sticky, her throat wanted to swallow on a gulp of nerves. And not—for that instant—because she was scared for her son.

"Serena?" His voice was like music, low and mystical. But where that magical tone had worked to calm her son, it had the opposite effect on her. "Did you see exactly what stung him? Whether it was a bee, hornet, wasp, what?"

"Yes, I saw it. As far as I could tell, it was just a plain old ground bee."

"Unusually strong reaction for just a plain old ground bee. Nate, do you remember if you were ever stung by a bee before today?"

"I guess. I don't remember 'xactly..."

Serena stepped in. "He's been stung twice. Once, when he was two years old. And another time last fall. He was miserable both times—who isn't miserable with a bee sting? But this time it was so much worse. He's all right, though, isn't he..." She refused to phrase that like a question.

"He will be."

She watched Blake impatiently push the stethoscope behind his neck, out of the way, and give a smile to her son that took her breath away. His strong, tanned hands circled Nate's wrists, taking his pulse without the little one knowing. "Do you happen to know if you're allergic to bee stings, sport?"

"I'm tough," Nate informed him.

"Hey, I can see that you're very tough and really strong. But you can be tough and strong and still be allergic to something."

"Well, I'm pretty sure I'm not 'llergic, because my mom woulda told me."

Blake hadn't looked at her again and didn't now. "Serena, is his father allergic?"

She gulped. Fast. "I don't know. I never happened to ask and the question just never came up."

"Okay. Let's go at the problem another way. Were each of the previous stings noticeably worse than the one before?"

"Yes. Yes, for absolute sure. The first one just welted up like a mosquito bite, really. But then the one he got last fall— I wasn't there. He was fishing with my two brothers. But by the time he got home, his leg was really swollen, and I thought maybe he'd been stung by a wasp instead of a bee, and no one knew. But this time—today—I was there. Right there. I had the stinger out in two shakes. I elevated his arm, had it cleaned and on ice so fast—"

"And yet he still had this reaction," Blake finished

for her. Again Serena watched him examine Nate, his fingers testing for swelling under his arms, on his throat, yet never losing his reassuring smile for her son. "Do you know how much you weigh, big guy?"

"A' course."

Blake grinned at the number. "Okay, and now can you tell me how old you are?"

"Sure. Six."

"Well, I could see what a strong, brave boy you were, but I still never guessed—" Something abruptly changed in his tone. Something sharp, something fast. "Six years old, huh?"

For maybe five seconds nothing seemed to move or breathe in the examining room. Blake could have been a marble statue, permanently carved in a bent posture over Nate. He never looked at her, never looked away from her son. He just didn't seem to be breathing for those few seconds.

"What's wrong?" Serena surged forward.

He acted as if he hadn't heard her. He just talked to Nate as if only the two of them were in the room. "Okay, Nate. You're pretty miserable, aren't you?"

"Yeah. It hurts. And I feel really awful."

"I know you do. But we're going to give you some medicine right now to help you feel better." Blake strode to the door, opened it, and said something quietly to the nurse. He was back at Nate's side in seconds. "This medicine is called an antihistamine. It's going to make you feel a little light-headed, but that's the worst of it, and that part will last only for a little while. After that, you might feel sleepy. That doesn't sound too bad, does it?"

"No. Can I go home then?"

"Well, let me tell you the plan. We're going to try that medicine as soon as the nurse brings it in, and then I want you to stay here for a little while because I want to make sure it works. If you start feeling better, it's an A-OK and you're outta here. But just in case that medicine isn't the best one for you, I want you to stick around for a few more minutes so I'll know it, because then I could try a different type of special medicine. You get me? One way or another, we're going to make sure you feel better. You okay with that plan?"

"Yeah. That sounds good." Or it did for a second. Serena knew her son, and sensed the instant Nate smelled a skunk in the woods. "Hey, you're not talking about giving me a shot, are you?"

"Yup." Blake's tone was smoother than butter. "And I have to tell you a secret, Nate. Don't tell your mom. Don't tell anyone, okay? But I really hate shots."

Nate's eyes had instantly welled, but now those tears hovered without falling. "You hate shots, too?"

"Oh, man. I sure do," Blake promised him.

"Well, me, too. And I really don't want one right now."

"I wouldn't, either," Blake said sympathetically. "You already had a terrible day. It's just not fair to have to get a shot, too, is it?"

"No, it's not."

"If it were me, now, I'd be conning my mom out of something I really wanted after a day like this." The nurse quietly walked in, and Blake smoothly blocked Nate's view of the needle as he kept talking. "Like a new book. Or a root beer float. Or getting to rent a movie you wanted to see. Something tells me that your mom is going to be real sympathetic this afternoon if you happen to want something. You being so brave and all, how can she resist? I haven't kept track, but were there some good movies that came out this summer?"

"Yeah, you bet. In fact..." Tears suddenly gushed from Nate's eyes. "Hey."

"Count to five, Nate. Then it'll be over. It's a fast one," Blake promised him. "And then I have to tell you and your mom something... There, see, it's all done. That's it. And now, just in case you feel a little woozy, lay there for me, okay? And listen." To the nurse, he murmured, "Thanks, Patrice."

When the nurse left the room, he met Serena's eyes. But his expression had completely changed. The first way he'd looked at her—that pulse-rocking, hormone-stirring, oh-man-how-great-to-see-you look—had disappeared. This was the cold-blue formal look he reserved for strangers.

"We're going to monitor Nate's pulse and blood pressure for a few minutes. My feeling is that the antihistamine is going to work just fine. But everything you told me about his history with bee stings leads me to believe that he has a cumulative allergic reaction going on here. I'm going to give you a prescription for an anaphylaxis emergency kit. What the kit contains is a shot, a single dose of epinephrine. Nate is probably too young to use it on himself, but I still want to include him. I want both of you to know how it's done and what symptoms we need to be watching for, just in case he gets stung another time.''

Serena concentrated through the whole conversation and demonstration. But a half hour later, as she drove home with Nate curled next to her on the truck seat, she couldn't stop remembering Blake's sudden change in attitude. Not toward her son. But definitely toward her.

She turned left on Willow Brook, zoomed through town to get to 17, then aimed west toward the Crazy Mountains. Only a few miles from home, she knew how much the meeting with Blake had affected her. Her heart was still drumming, her palms still slick with anxiety.

She tried to concentrate on driving. A stretch of brilliant fireweed blossoms blanketed the mountain meadow to her north. The south valley, though, was fenced for pasture. Blue larkspur poked up around the fence, and the rolling green-brown graze land was sliced by a skinny stream that caught the diamond sunlight every now and then. Cattle grazed, looking half asleep. Someone's tractor raised plumes of dust from a quarter mile away. Then there was nothing, all signs of traffic and people disappearing when she took the last turn toward home.

And still her heart was pounding.

Part of the problem, Serena assured herself, was simply the shock of finding Blake in Whitehorn. She'd never expected to see him again at all.

Seven years ago, when Blake had left for California, she'd known he'd never planned to return to Montana—and for darn sure, he'd never wanted to practice medicine anywhere near a small town. In all those years they hadn't seen or spoken to each other. They'd been friends—more than friends—which had made it inappropriate for her to contact him again once she'd heard he was engaged.

The thing was, though, today he'd initially seemed warmly and honestly happy to see her. Until halfway through the conversation.

You're not one to borrow trouble, she reminded herself. He was being businesslike. Doctorlike. He gave all his attention to Nate, which is exactly what he was supposed to do, exactly what you wanted him to do. His behavior never had to mean that something was suddenly wrong...

But there was, she feared.

Oh, God, there was.

"I'm never going back to him, Mom," Nate suddenly piped up, his voice fretful and groggy.

"Oh?" Ahead, she could see their place. The yard was an oasis of cool shade. Squirrels scampered between the horse chestnut trees lining the driveway.

Behind the house she could see the stand of paper birch, their trunks so white, their leaves fluttering in the sunlit wind, and curving further back was her pride-and-joy water garden, which, unfortunately, had turned into the pride and joy for deer, raccoon, jack-rabbits and every other critter that wanted a cool rest stop from time to time. Whiskey recognized the truck and barked a greeting, but the old red setter was too lazy to get up. One black-and-white-spotted stray kitten was curled up under Whiskey's paw.

Animals kept showing up at her doorstep. She couldn't understand it.

She turned into the drive, and swiftly cut the engine with a studied look at her son. "If you still feel dizzy, I can carry you in, lovebug. And what's this, you didn't like Dr. Blake? I thought you guys were getting on pretty well."

"Yeah, at first. But he gave me a shot. Dr. Carey doesn't give me shots. I'm never going back to him— Quit it, Mom, I can walk. Sheesh."

She was willing to let Nate walk into the house under his own steam. But she ran around to his side of the truck and stayed closer than arm's length, just in case. "Nate, I thought you understood what was happening there. You needed the shot, because you had a serious reaction to the bee sting. Dr. Blake was just doing what any good doctor would have done. If Dr. Carey had been there, she'd have done the same thing."

"I don't care. I'm never going to back to the doctor's as long as I live. Any doctor. And nobody can make me.''

It was going to be a long evening, Serena thought dryly. Nate was the most perfect son a mother could have. Priceless, precious and precocious. But when he didn't feel well—no different than any other male—he liked every female in his vicinity to pay, and preferably to pay big.

Two more cats pounced when they stepped inside. Nuisance was a white Persian who'd walked in three years before and refused to leave, and George was a scrawny calico who'd had kittens this spring in spite of impossible odds.

''Are you thirsty, Nate? And how's the tummy—could you eat anything?''

''I want to go get the Wild Warriors game.''

''And we'll do that, tomorrow. I promise. But I'm not about to take you shopping when you don't feel well.''

''I feel fine. And I want Wild Warriors. Why can't I have it now? Why?'' Her son glared at her with blurry eyes, so dizzy he didn't even know he was swaying. ''My arm hurts. And I don't love you anymore. I did, but now I don't. I'll p'bably never love you again. You let that horrible doctor give me a shot.''

Even in his terrible two's, Nate had never pulled tantrums on her. His temperament had always been happy, always loving toward animals, always patient and gentle by nature. But when he was sick, nobody or nothing was going to sway him out of being testy.

Serena ran and kept running. She brought him lemonade—doctored up with a cherry—turned on the VCR to his favorite movie, made mac and cheese because that was sacred food to her son, fetched Whiskey, Nuisance, and two toys from the bedroom that he wanted next to him on the couch.

Around eight he finally dozed off, and as she carried him into his bedroom, he was snoring little-boy breathy snores, snuggled against her shoulder. It was still daylight. She laid him down, cuddled Brer Rabbit next to his tummy, then soothed the dinosaur sheets around his chin, tucking everything in. Carefully. The alligators could get in unless the covers were tucked just so—which Nate had explained to her many, many times—so the proper kind of tucking-in was a mom job that Serena took very seriously.

Afterward, she anticipated hurling herself on the couch and crashing in front of a mindless sitcom. Not only was she beat, but the moments after Nate went to sleep were invariably the most peaceful ones in her day.

Not tonight. Restlessly she prowled from window to window, thinking she wanted a shower and a mug of tea and just some plain old quiet time, yet unable to settle down to doing anything. Except pace.

Her home had always soothed her—not that anything about the place was fancy. Seven years ago Serena could have found some way to stay in medical school if material riches had mattered to her, but thankfully she'd discovered how much she loved teaching, and her teacher's salary stretched all she needed it to. The house was an L-shaped ranch. The farthest room in the back was her bedroom, followed by a bath, then Nate's room, then a third bedroom they used as a study, and then the huge kitchen that took up the seat of the L. Down a few steps from the kitchen was an open living area, with a circular brick fireplace plunked in the middle.

For so many years Serena had never thought about having Cheyenne blood, yet lately she kept noticing her heritage showing up in so many unconscious ways. She'd chosen cinnamon and vanilla colors, clay floors, lots of light, lots of plants. The deck outside her bedroom doors was where she and Nate fed critters and puttered and grew things. Their kitchen table was a long pine slab where they rarely had room to eat, because—like today—they were building volcanoes and crystal gardens and waiting for the latest shaving-cream pictures to dry.

Absently Serena tugged off the band that held her braid together and started finger-threading the long strands loose. Her hair reached almost to her waist. An inappropriate length for a woman her age, she thought, but she was too blasted vain to cut it. During the day she always pinned or braided it, anyway. It was just now, the end of the day, when she let it loose. She fetched a brush and started working it through as, from the west porch, she watched the sun start to set.

She remembered when her parents died. She'd been almost four. One morning her mom and dad were there, everything to her, and that afternoon a grand-parent-aged white couple—strangers—had come to pick up her and her two older brothers. Over the years folks had asked her if it wasn't confusing, being Cheyenne and being raised white. But it never had been. Not for her. She'd never felt any particular ties to the nearby Native American reservation, yet on the inside she'd always felt content and secure, being Native. Her sensitivity toward nature and the earth, and the spirituality of being that renewed her—those things were all Cheyenne. Yet love was love, and she'd been so deeply and positively loved by her adoptive family that she often thought of herself as white, too. For Serena, there was no contradiction.

The only negative she felt from her growing-up years was an awareness of how hard her foster family had struggled to support her. She hated being beholden. The home she'd made for Nate, with Nate, reflected all those parts of her. A respect for nature. A love for growing things. A need to possess only those things that she really loved, really used. The chunk of sapphire—native to the Montana mountain country—on the coffee table in front of her was testament to that part of her. She'd never wanted a fancy necklace, only the stone as it was found in nature.

She picked up the sapphire and plunked it down

again. She tried rebrushing her hair, then fitfully tossed the brush down, too. All the things that normally comforted and soothed her weren't working tonight. The only thing she could think about—and worry about—was Blake Remmington.

And somehow, when she heard the rap on her door at the first hush of night, she knew who her caller had to be. And her heart leaped—with both fear and anticipation.

# Two

Blake rapped on Serena's door a second time, then stepped back and waited. So typical of a Montana summer, the early August night was hot and dry. Unbreathably hot. And parch-your-throat dry. Still, holding the weather responsible for his mood was like blaming a rattlesnake for being temperamental.

Stay calm, he kept telling himself. But he felt hot, edgy, and strung tighter than a rubber band threatening to snap. This whole year had been one nonstop crisis after another. Three months before, he'd come back to Whitehorn because of a phone call from Garrett Kincaid—a man who should have been a stranger but instead had turned out to be his real grandfather. That was the first emotional bomb. Then came the shock of realizing that the man he'd called "Dad" his entire life was no kin at all. Worse yet was discovering that his real father was Garrett's son, Larry, a philandering womanizer who'd not only cheated repeatedly on his wife, but left bastards in his wake the way Hansel and Gretel trailed breadcrumbs. A trail that included Blake and his twin brother, Trent.

Lately Blake felt as if he'd fallen down Alice's

rabbit hole—only this wasn't Wonderland. For thirty-two years he'd believed certain things about himself and his life, and now he discovered they were all lies. He couldn't seem to stop feeling blindsided and confused.

A few weeks back when Carey Hall Kincaid had invited him to join her pediatrics practice, he'd leaped at the idea, thinking that if he stayed in Whitehorn for a while he could glue the pieces of his life back together, figure out where he belonged, get down to the truth.

But then he'd re-met Serena that afternoon.

If his life had been blindsided by a few emotional bombs before, they now seemed like nothing. Pipsqueak trouble. Seeing her again had knocked him off his feet.

He rapped on her front door again, then shifted impatiently on his feet. She was home. She had to be. Her aging red pickup was parked in the drive, her son was sick and it was almost nine o'clock. All the evidence added up—she was here for sure.

He glanced around, thinking that the place reminded him so much of Serena that it hurt. The house was a far drive from town, chunked down in the middle of nowhere, a private slice of heaven with a rolling, dipping landscape out her back door and a breathtaking view of the Crazy Mountains. When he'd first stepped out of his black Acura, an Irish setter with graying whiskers had immediately loped toward him. A real heroic watchdog, the setter had walked toward

Serena's door and then promptly flopped onto his back for a tummy rub. Now a cat showed up. A mangy calico with a crackly purr and a scarred ear, who refused to quit winding seductively around his legs. He sneezed. Damn cat only rubbed harder.

Stay cool, he told himself. Stay cool, stay calm. Do the right thing.

Blake wanted to handle this coming confrontation in the right way, but seeing this place just reminded him of how Serena used to be. A hopeless critter lover. A helpless sunset addict. She was a nature lover from the get-go, the kind of girl who'd run barefoot in dew-drenched grass, lick the rain with her tongue, and was just always happy. Natural. Easy to be with.

Remembering made it hard to hold on to his tight, edgy, angry mood…and then Serena was suddenly there, standing in the doorway. Taking his breath away. Just looking at her made him even more roiled up and unsettled.

The lamplight behind her highlighted that exquisite profile, the proud cheekbones, the tender mouth. She'd undone the tidy braid from this afternoon and her hair was now a loose shower of raven-black silk swaying way past her shoulder blades. No man could look at that hair and not want to touch. She'd never said her exact height, but he'd always figured it around five-seven—tall enough yet she was so lithe, so slight, so light on her feet that she could walk up to a deer without making a sound. Blake had seen it happen.

And those liquid brown eyes of hers had turned him into butter before. Hot butter. When push came to shove, everything about Serena turned him on—and had from the instant he'd laid eyes on her.

Still, seven years ago, he'd been twenty-five—a boy, really, a man untried in life. He should have long gotten over his adolescent hormonal response to her. Obviously he was wrong. But hell, he seemed to be wrong about everything in his life right now, so what was new?

"Blake?" She pushed open the screen to let him in. "I heard the knock, but I thought I imagined the sound. I can't believe it's you out here. Whiskey, let him by."

The Irish setter was not only a complete failure as a watchdog but switched loyalties without a qualm. He ignored Serena's command and hurled himself in front of Blake's path, apparently filled with exuberant hope that he'd get his tummy scratched again. Another cat showed up, a hoity-toity white Persian, prancing around as if waiting for him to acknowledge royalty—or risk getting tripped. Even a saint would be hard-pressed to maintain a serious mood, but damn, there was nothing humorous about this visit—or his situation. "I realize I should have called before stopping by, Serena. But I just wanted to be sure that Nate was okay."

Almost as quickly as she met his eyes, her gaze shied swiftly away. She scooped up the cat, tried to push Whiskey out of his way, and once the whole group had been herded inside, closed the screen door. "Nate's much better. Your stopping by is way beyond the call of duty, but I'm glad you did. It's just good to see you again. I was so worried about Nate this afternoon that there just wasn't a chance to ask how you were, how life's been treating you. Listen, could I get you something to drink?"

"Yeah, if you have something cold and it isn't too much trouble. Is he asleep?"

"Yes. In fact, the medicine hit him like a sledgehammer."

Again, Blake felt knocked for six. Her easy welcome was just like old times, her natural smile the last thing he'd expected. There seemed no worry in her expression, no hint of guilt.

"Well, some grogginess is a normal side effect of the medicine. With any luck, he'll sleep soundly through the night. But as long as I'm here, I'll check in on him—if you don't mind."

"Heavens, of course I don't mind."

By the time she'd led him through the house to the boy's bedroom, Blake figured he'd seen the whole house except for her sleeping area. The inside struck him as just as unsettling as the outside—and for the same reason. It stabbed his nerves how much he remembered about Serena, and how much the place had her personal stamp, from the circular hearth in the living room to the heaped projects in the kitchen to the colors, the coral of clay and bark-browns and splashes of natural turquoise. Most people used coffee tables for books. She used hers for a collection of crusty rocks—sapphires, amethysts, geodes, crystals, garnets. All raw stones, nothing made into jewelry or necessarily of gem quality, but the facets caught the lamplight and made the jewels glow. Plants bloomed in the room wherever there was light, waterfalls of green splashing from every surface. Kids' toys were liberally strewn around.

Damn. The whole place reminded him of how comfortable they'd been as friends back in medical school, the dozens of times he'd stopped by just because being with her had always been so easy. Back then her place was cluttered, but always with such strange, interesting stuff, a haven where he could put up his feet and never feel stressed or as if he had to put on the dog.

Tonight, though, he didn't want to see or think anything positive about Serena. Still, for a few seconds, that particular problem completely disappeared from his mind. The instant he walked into Nate's room, he felt an emotional slug direct to his heart.

Even in the shadowed room, he could make out whale wallpaper, dinosaur sheets and Lego rockets on the dresser. While the living room had a clay-tile floor, she'd carpeted her son's room with a thick, luxuriously soft rug. And the boy himself... Blake couldn't see him clearly, but somewhere in all the stuffed animals crowding the bed was hair with a distinctive cowlick and the specific shape of a nose and chin and forehead. Again Blake felt his heart clutch. And then slam.

Carefully he tiptoed closer. Nate didn't waken, didn't even stir when he took the boy's pulse and felt that small forehead for a temperature. Once Blake had assured himself the boy was all right, he meant to exit quickly—he really didn't want to wake the tyke—yet somehow he found himself frozen for a moment, then two, unable to tear his eyes from Nate, aware Serena stood in the doorway behind him and had to be curious why he was still standing there in the dark.

Eventually he turned around. He felt Serena staring at his face, studying him, but she could not have seen his expression with the room so draped in darkness. She led him back down the hall to the kitchen, where she paused to fill two glasses with sun tea and ice cubes and sprigs of mint.

From nowhere she said very quietly, "You think it's about time we both tried being honest? You could have called if all you'd wanted to know was how Nate was responding to the medication. You had another reason for stopping by."

"You've got that dead right." When she handed him the glass, he took several long gulps, because he was afraid his throat was so dry—or he was so damn furious—that he wouldn't be able to talk. "Let's go outside."

"I don't want to be out of hearing range of Nate."

"I understand. But I don't want to be where the

boy could hear raised voices and be frightened by
them, either.''

She sucked in a wary breath, but then simply motioned him through the living room and out the front
door again. Naturally, the whole blasted menagerie of
misfit critters had to follow her. Outside, she sat on
the porch step, leaving room for him to sit next to
her.

He'd noticed her nonstop since he'd arrived, yet
sitting next to her was different. Before, he hadn't
been conscious of her bare feet, the sarong-style
denim skirt that showed off her long brown legs, the
scooped white T-shirt that loosely, intimately, cupped
her breasts. Her choice of clothing was cool and comfortable, nothing fancy. They looked purely feminine
on her. Pure woman. Like her. And her voice was
softer than a lover's whisper. ''You're angry, aren't
you, Blake?''

''I'm not sure 'angry' begins to cut it. How about
totally furious?'' He paused to take a calming breath
and the damn dog promptly pushed a wet nose into
his palm—as if he were in any mood to pet a critter.
Then the prissy Persian put a paw on his thigh, as if
expecting him to create space on his lap for her. He
needed to concentrate to keep his cool, and the blasted
zoo wasn't helping. ''Serena, I happen to be allergic
to bee stings. The same kind of allergy that Nate has.
The kind that I told you is commonly inherited.''

''I didn't know about your allergy.''

''You had no reason to. The subject never came up

in the time we knew each other. But that's not the point," he said impatiently. "Even if the bee sting allergy had never come up, I could see right off that Nate may have inherited his good looks from you but he never got that square chin or the shape of his head from you."

"No, he definitely didn't," she agreed softly.

"He's my son, isn't he, damn it?"

One word. Again, gently, softly said. "Yes."

He surged to his feet as if someone had jabbed him with an electric pole. Somehow the shock was even worse than this afternoon, when, yes, of course he'd figured it out. God knew he hadn't been anticipating trouble when she'd walked in. He'd barely been able to take his eyes off her, he'd been so glad to see her, feeling a curl of vital awareness and aliveness such as he hadn't felt since…hell, since the last time he'd been with Serena years before.

But the age and look of her son had kept distracting him. The boy's facial features had distracted him even more, until even someone trying to deny the truth as exuberantly as he was couldn't keep burying his head in the sand. Still, sensing the truth and having her openly admit it were two different things. "How could you not tell me? How could you do this to me, to him? Why the hell didn't you talk to me when you first realized you were pregnant?"

Her lips parted as if she wanted to answer him, but her gaze suddenly lit on his face, searching his expression and eyes, as if seeking some way to reply.

He didn't want some tactful, thought-out answer. What he really wanted was to smash his fist into a wall—but there wasn't one handy. "For God's sake, Serena, it's not like we were enemies. I thought we were friends. Good friends. I can't think of any reason why you'd have been afraid to tell me. Did you think I wouldn't come through? Wouldn't marry you? That I'd have deserted you without any help if I'd known you were pregnant?"

"Oh, Blake...you're so upset."

"Of course I'm upset! I just found out that I have a six-year-old son!"

How was it, Serena thought painfully, that the people you cared about the most were somehow the ones you managed to hurt the worst? Her heart ached. She'd never have willingly hurt Blake. Never.

Telling him about Nate had just never seemed a simple thing seven years ago—or now.

Impatiently she snapped her fingers, because Whiskey and George and Nuisance were all snuzzling under his palm to get petted, competing for his attention. The animals all sensed that this was a terribly unhappy human who needed comfort. So did she.

When the animals realized she meant business, they backed off and settled down. But she couldn't. She had no idea how to handle Blake. He was still six feet, two inches of towering, injured man who was glowering in the darkness like lightning about to explode.

"You have every right to be upset—with the situation, and with me," she said quietly. "It was wrong not to tell you. Terribly wrong. But I made the best choice I knew how to at the time, Blake. The truth is I didn't know what to do. And then time passed. And the more time passed, I just couldn't imagine picking up a phone and dropping news like this on you out of the blue."

"The question is, why you didn't tell me from the get-go. You got pregnant and I was the father. Where's the complication in that equation? I had a right to know."

"Yes. You did." It was just terribly hard to think straight when he was so mad. Eyes-colder-than-ice mad. Shoulders-rigid-as-marble mad. She had no fear that Blake would hurt her, ever, but she did think his mood was disturbingly unpredictable at the moment.

But so was hers. In fact, she'd been having regular galloping heart attacks since last May—she hadn't seen Blake or known he was coming back to Whitehorn then, but that was when the Kincaid scandal broke in town and she'd heard that Blake Remmington was one of the illegitimate Kincaid heirs. Everyone knew Larry Kincaid had played around, but no one guessed until after his death how many bastard children he'd fathered. Normally Serena never listened to gossip, but she knew it would kill Blake to find out who sired him.

One of the reasons she'd fallen so hopelessly in love with Blake back in medical school was that, at the core, he was so old-fashioned. A man who really believed in honor. A guy who honest-to-Pete lived by a code. Discovering that he was sired by an irresponsible womanizer like Larry Kincaid had had to hurt him terribly. And Serena understood perfectly why he was so extra upset right now, as well. Finding out about Nate was a huge shock in itself, but worse yet was Blake discovering that he had an illegitimate son—not long after he'd discovered he was one himself.

She wanted to explain. She needed to explain. But Serena wasn't positive that Blake would hear anything she said right now. He was pacing around her front yard in the pitch dark like a wounded panther, stalking the shadows, then the light, unable to stand still, maybe hoping that all that pacing would stop him from punching something. Obviously, though, she had to try to communicate, whether it was a worthless effort or not. "I was wrong."

"More than wrong, Serena!"

"All right. More than wrong." Her eyes tracked him, wishing she could see even the smallest sign of his calming down. There wasn't one. "Do you remember, Blake? We were both in medical school. Both exhausted all the time from our schedules."

"Yeah, so?"

"So that was when your mom died, and you came back from the funeral even more exhausted. You wouldn't talk about it. Not with me. Not with anyone, as far as I knew. But you looked like there was a raw sore inside you that just kept bleeding.''

"Damn it, Serena! Of course I remember when my mother died. And yeah, I was torn up. But what does that have to do with Nate, or with your not telling me that we had a son together?''

She whispered, "I was in love with you. Years before that. But you didn't feel the same way. It's not like there was a problem. When we ran across each other, you always treated me like a friend, someone you were glad to see, glad to talk to…but that was all. Except that one time, Blake, that one night. I just wanted to be there for you. To love you. To help you through the grieving. You didn't seduce me. I was the one who was responsible, who came on to you. You weren't expecting anything to happen.''

"No, I wasn't. But it wasn't like you planned it, either. Neither of us expected that night to happen.''

Her mind suddenly filled with the memories. No, she hadn't expected anything sexual to happen, but once she'd offered that first kiss, they'd fallen on each other as if two lit fuses were connecting to the same stick of dynamite. Once lit, nothing was going to stop that bomb from exploding. She said patiently, "Whatever I expected or didn't, it was still my choice, my responsibility for starting something. I never wanted you to feel any kind of obligation. I wanted to make love with you. It wasn't your fault.''

Blake threw up his hands. "Because you offered the first kiss, you think you have more fault? That's like adding one and one and thinking three is the answer. If I'd just known you were pregnant—"

She finished the sentence for him. "—you would have asked me to marry you. I know. In fact, I never doubted that for even a second."

He looked even more confounded. "Then why didn't you tell me?"

"Actually, I tried to tell you," she said quietly. "It was eight weeks later before I'd taken a pregnancy test and knew. And I went over to your place as soon as I found out. Do you remember a night when it was cold and windy and wild and pouring buckets, you were having cold pizza for dinner—"

"Yeah, yeah, so?"

God, he was so impatient. Still so furious. She wrapped her arms around her body, hugging herself for warmth, even though the night was still balmy. "You were happy to see me when I stopped by," she recalled.

"We were friends. Of course I was happy to see you. The only reason we hadn't seen each other more often was because our work schedules were so full."

"But you were extra happy that night because you'd won the residency in California, the one you'd applied for in Los Angeles and really wanted. You never wanted to come back to Whitehorn to live. You never wanted a small town practice. The L.A. offer was everything you'd worked for and dreamed of. And by then...well, I'd heard there was a woman in your life."

For the first time she saw him hesitate, frown, look not so sure of his ground. "Elaine."

"The woman you eventually married."

"I wasn't married then, Serena. I hadn't known her that long then. And nothing would have happened between me and Elaine if I'd realized that you were pregnant."

"Well, how I saw it, Blake, was that my telling would have ruined everything. All your dreams. All the things that were finally going right for you. You were never close with Trent, even if he was your twin brother. Or your dad—and I don't mean Larry Kincaid, but Harold Remmington, the man you believed was your dad when you were growing up. So there was just your mom, and when she died, that just left you so alone. You paid your own way, took every step alone, expected nothing from anyone. But it was hard, and finally, finally things were starting to come together for you." She lifted a hand in a gesture that asked for understanding. "I wanted you to have that shot at happiness. I didn't want to screw it up."

"You're making it sound like your life wasn't suddenly screwed up by an unexpected pregnancy."

"Actually, it wasn't, Blake. It changed things, of course. I couldn't handle med school and a pregnancy both, but I also discovered that I never really wanted to be a doctor. Not like you did. I already had all the science credits, so all I needed was some education courses to get my teaching degree. And I love teaching. The hours are wonderful for Nate, too. And my two older brothers are crazy about him, so it wasn't like he never had strong male influences in his life.''

"Serena, I'm not doubting that you've been a great mom or that you've given him a great life. But your silence meant I never had a chance to be his dad.''

With her heart feeling heavier than lead, she pushed a hand through her hair and closed her eyes for a second's breath. "I understand. And it's been on my heart. That you had the right to know. But as many times as I can apologize, and as bad as I feel that I never told you earlier, all I can say is the truth. At the time I made the best decision I was capable of making. You would have offered to marry me. A Native American woman—and I didn't know how you felt about that. A woman whose roots were in Whitehorn—a place I understood that you never wanted to live. And then there was the bottom line: you didn't love me, Blake.''

"Maybe not. But you were my friend and I thought a lot of you. Love could have come.''

She shook her head, fiercely, fast. For an instant images of her childhood tore loose like trapped bubbles surging to the surface of the sea.

Losing her parents had been the most awful thing in her universe, but she'd been blessed by folks and family who loved her. She'd learned to embrace life because of her foster family, but it had always scraped on her heart. The feeling of being beholden, of being taken in by a good family who couldn't afford her. They'd been extra poor and had to struggle nonstop because of her and her brothers. She remembered their always going without, but even more, she remembered feeling helpless to do anything about it.

It was a feeling she couldn't stand as a child. Or now. "I wouldn't marry you or anyone because you felt beholden or responsible."

He'd quit pacing and was just standing there, a leg cocked forward, moonlight showering his shoulders. Now he frowned. "I don't know what you mean. A child *is* a responsibility."

"Yes. But love isn't. Or it shouldn't be."

He shook his head, as if exasperated with diverting down this side road when the main highway points were getting lost. "I don't get you. To me, love and responsibility are part of the same package. And back to something else you said. What'd you mean by that Native American comment?"

"I believe the woman you married was a blue-eyed blonde," she said honestly.

"The woman who I divorced was a blue-eyed blonde. And are you trying to seriously tick me off? We were friends. You think I judged you in some lesser way because of your being Cheyenne?"

"No, no. I'd never accuse you of prejudice that way, Blake. That wasn't what I meant at all. I was just trying to be honest." She hesitated, grappling for the right words. "Seven years ago I might as well have been a hundred years younger. In some ways I really grew up naive. Because I was raised by white foster parents, I honestly had no concept that my being Native American was an issue for some people. It took going to college to get the idea that some anglo guys assumed my morals were freer because I was Native American.''

''Serena! I never thought that about you! Nor would anyone who even knew you longer than two minutes!''

''I believe you. But all I'm trying to say is, that until I grew up, I honestly had no comprehension what different cultures meant to some people. And that's one of the things that troubled me when I got pregnant. Again, I didn't want you to feel like you had to do something out of responsibility. Because there was that extra problem, too. I don't know how you could have leaped into a relationship with anyone, with me, without needing time to think about the race thing.''

''You are trying to tick me off.'' His growl wasn't unlike Whiskey's.

''Marrying someone who's different is a serious thing.''

''Well, of course it is. But we'd known each other for years. It's not like either of us is 'different' in any way that matters.''

The comment was so like him, Serena mused, and suddenly felt hormones singing, stinging, through her pulse just like years ago. The damn man. Blake was a rule-lover while she ran her life freestyle; he was contained where she was emotional. They were never alike. She'd never wanted to fall in love with someone tuned to such a completely different channel. But as bullheaded as Blake could be, he was also good, deep down in his soul. No way he'd let something paltry, such as race or religion, get in the way of his standing up for what he knew was right. It would never occur to Blake that a good man would do otherwise. And everything he'd said reminded her in so many desperate, wonderful ways of why she'd first fallen in love with him.... But that wasn't getting their problems handled.

"Blake..." She hesitated. "More than once over the years, I wanted to call you. It's sat on my conscience all this time, that for your sake, and Nate's, this should never have been a long-term secret. But until recently, when you came home after Larry Kincaid died, I assumed you were married and settled happily in California. And I felt the same about that— I didn't want you in my life or in Nate's life only because you felt an obligation."

Something got through to him—maybe her tone, more than what she said. But the belligerence finally seemed to sink out of his shoulders. He scraped a hand through his hair and blew out a sigh. "Finding out so suddenly that I'm a father... I just feel...pole-axed," he admitted.

"Yes."

"I don't know what I should say or do."

"Yes." She understood that, too. And how badly not having those answers would drive Blake bananas.

"Hell." He heaved another sigh. "Look, whatever

we did or failed to do before, neither of us can change that. It's spilled milk. But I want to do the right thing now. For you. For our son.''

As if it were happening to someone else, she felt herself standing up, felt her bare feet in the cool grass as they moved toward him.

*Obviously you're not going to kiss him,* her conscience informed her, as if the idea were laughable, completely out of the question. Which, of course, it was.

She'd made love with Blake once. Years before. He was angry with her now, and for good reasons. In fact, there was nothing between them right now but a painful and terribly sensitive problem.

But, oh, God, that was exactly why. Why she'd made love with him that once. Why she'd never been able to stop herself from falling in love with him.

And just maybe, why no man had even come close to her heart the same way since.

Blake had always set impossible standards for himself. He never made a mistake if he could prevent it, never asked for help from anyone, never let on that he had fears the way all mortals did.

But it was the mortal man who'd gone to her head years before. And who still did now.

She saw the frown pleat his forehead, saw his head cock in an expression of curiosity and confusion. He didn't understand what she was doing, what on earth had motivated her to suddenly stand up and fly toward him.

He figured it out. When she surged up on tiptoe, when she cupped her palms around his head to pull him down. When her lips took his, in an eyes-closed, need-to-do-this kiss. Oh, he got it, all right. His whole body froze, as if a monster just wandered into the yard and he couldn't believe what he was seeing.

He stood still. But not forever. Eventually his mouth remembered her mouth. His taste remembered her taste. So maybe it had only been that once, but that night had changed her life, changed every idea she'd ever had about sensuality and sex and giving and men, exploded every concept she'd ever felt about control and good-girl behavior and morality. Because nothing had mattered to her that night but him. His aching, lonely kisses. His reverent kisses. His wild, rough, to-hell-with-everything-I-want-you-now kisses.

That was precisely how she felt at this moment. In the span of a heartbeat, everything changed. The real world hadn't disappeared. She could still smell sweet grass and primroses and the minty iced tea on his breath. She could still hear the cackle of crickets and the cat purring—the cat never stopped purring—and through the screen door, the muted canned laughter from a left-on TV program.

Yet the only sensory perceptions really denting her awareness had his name on them. His smooth, sleek muscles, the way they bunched under her hands. His mouth, taking her under like an ocean current gathering power. The heat coming off his skin, coming off hers.

Need sparked like the flame of a match, the burn so sudden, so bright, so unexpected. A moan whispered in the darkness. The dog, she thought—but it wasn't the dog. It was her. An instinctively angry moan, that no man had touched her this way in so long, that no other man seemed to move her the way Blake did. That wasn't how she wanted it. It was never how she expected her life to be. Still, she remembered that stinging, vibrant excitement humming through her blood, the dizzying high, the delicious, wicked sensation of being pulled in by him, to him, kissed until she couldn't breathe, kissed as if he'd die if he couldn't have her.

He suddenly jerked away from her faster than a cat in a thunderstorm. "Damn it, Serena." His hands closed around her shoulders, his elbows locked straight as if to force a distance between them. "I never meant to..."

He dropped his hands completely then and backed up another foot.

"Take it easy," she said softly.

"No. Neither of us is going to take it easy. We're going to do the right thing." Blake sounded absolutely dead sure of this, until his eyes suddenly rolled to the sky, and he muttered, "As soon as the two of us figure out whatever the hell that is."

# Three

Blake had never lacked decisiveness. But four days later he discovered that kissing a woman had completely destroyed—along with his ability to think—his skill at taking charge in a crisis. All those things he'd always taken for granted were gone. Poof. No hope of getting any of them back.

Something rocket-fast and diapered shrieked at the top of its lungs. Two teenagers jostled him, both carrying boxes that literally boomed at ear-shattering volumes. A maniacal battery-driven cackle echoed from the next aisle. A troop of small boys charged toward him with bloodthirsty war cries.

The whole milieu of the toy store could have been lots of fun, but not today. Blake pushed a harried hand through his hair. It was just eleven o'clock. He still had plenty of time to get to Serena's house before noon, but he needed a toy first. He needed one bad.

The problem was that it had to be the right toy, the perfect toy, and even though he'd been prowling through Bubba's Toy Store since it opened on Saturday—9:30 a.m., a lifetime ago—he just couldn't seem to decide on the right one.

It wasn't as if this were a test, he kept telling himself. All he'd had to do was ask, and Serena had readily agreed that he could spend time with Nate. She'd simply requested that he wait—for all their sakes—before revealing his fatherhood relationship. He concurred completely. Suddenly discovering that an honorless philanderer like Larry Kincaid was his real father had been a slap in the face for Blake; he never wanted to do that to his own son. He had no intention of telling Nate anything unless and until it was good for the boy. But the only way to prove himself to the child was to spend serious time with him.

Technically, that's all that was happening today. There was no noose tightening around his neck, no stress, all he was doing was going over to Serena's to hang out for a couple of hours. That's all. No sweat. No test. He just thought it'd break the ice with Nate if he brought a little something with him. Something like a toy.

Preferably the perfect toy.

Only what the Sam Hill did a six-year-old want? He loved kids and saw tons of them in the examining room every day. But that wasn't the same thing as playing with them. Were yo-yos too hard? If he bought something as expensive as a train set, would the kid think he was trying to buy his affection? Of course he was trying to wow his son, but he didn't want it to look that way. Some of the water pistols looked really cool, but guns were out. Serena'd probably have a cow about any toy resembling a weapon, he figured. Board games....

Aha. His gaze narrowed on the board games, again, but this time he saw potential. He could play with Nate if he bought him a game that took two players. That'd help them talk, get to know each other, and it wouldn't seem so much like bribery. He could just act as though he really wanted to play. He started squinting at the labels. War Zones.... Scrabble.... Candyland....

Finally—once that life-threatening decision had been made—he strode outside, expecting to feel better. Instead, another life-threatening problem charged into his mind. Serena. Kisses he'd been trying to forget replayed in his memory. Emotions he'd been practicing denying seeped back to the surface of his nerves. A night from seven years ago, never forgotten, never buried the way a man who'd been married should have buried such a recollection, ignited his hormones like a match to dry tinder.

A fat droplet spattered onto his head, helpfully distracting him. A serious rain would make the local ranchers deliriously happy—they'd been wringing hands for weeks about the drought, as if a dry August in Montana was something new. Weathermen had forecast a serious deluge for tonight, but right now the dribbles coming from the sky only added humidity to a tropically hot morning. Juggling his package, he wove around pedestrians, recognizing a few from years ago—Homer Gilmore, who had a habit of miraculously spotting aliens; Gracie Donahue, the buxom-mom-type lady who ran the local styling salon; Lettie Brownbear, a sweet old Cheyenne woman who rarely came near town. Clipping down Center Avenue, trying to remember where he'd parked his Acura, he suddenly spotted another familiar face.

But this particular face was more than passing familiar.

Bolting out of the Hip Hop Café was a man who measured a precise six feet, two inches. Athletic build. Dark brown hair, blue eyes.

Blake could have glanced in a mirror and seen the same thing, with a few minor differences. His twin brother walked like a lazy rogue, his hair was long enough to brush his collar and the clothes were notably less buttoned-down and more casual than Blake's. Growing up, people used to label Trent as the "maverick bad twin" and Blake as the "saint twin"—tags that both of them equally resented.

Trent spotted him at the same time Blake stopped on the sidewalk.

Blake almost smiled.

Trent almost smiled.

Hell, it was better than they used to get along. Blake switched the toy bag to his left hand and shot out his right. "I keep thinking, what's the point of us both being in Whitehorn when we seem to see each other even less? How's married life going? You treating my new sister-in-law okay?"

"I guess. Gina seems to be enjoying being pregnant. I've been meaning to call you, just to find out if you'd be willing to take on another patient a few months from now."

"There's always room in my practice for my niece or nephew." Blake grinned. "And I keep meaning to call to ask you and Gina over to dinner, but I still don't have much of a place put together. The move here was pretty rushed. How's Garrett?"

"He's fine." Trent hesitated. "It still feels like a shock. I still can't get used to thinking of him as our grandfather."

"Yeah. I know."

Both of them fell silent. Not a comfortable silence, Blake thought, but at least it wasn't like the fighting and animosity that had hounded their childhood. Shoppers brushed past them. Traffic ambled by. An occasional drip splashed down from the smoky gray sky.

Blake couldn't remember ever actually wanting to talk with his brother the way he wanted to now. Everything had been different between them since Garrett Kincaid had contacted them both in early May and revealed that he was their real grandfather. Before, the brothers had been like Mutt and Jeff. Trent was a wildcatter; Blake, a respectable pediatrician. Echoing how they'd always been: Trent had always been the wild one, the daredevil-rogue and, truth to tell, the exciting risk-anything kind of man Blake had always wanted to be. But Blake was only now coming to understand why they'd fought so much.

The whole truth about Larry Kincaid's life still wasn't known—and maybe never would be—but both brothers now knew certain facts, specifically that Larry had seduced their mother. She'd gotten pregnant with twins from the liaison. She'd married Harold Remmington early in that pregnancy, but God knew if Harold was really fooled as to whether he'd actually fathered the twins.

At this point Blake suspected that Harold must have guessed the truth, because he'd never seemed to be able to express love for either him or Trent. Blake and Trent had endured the same childhood. Their mother had been ambitious and overly busy, but at least she'd been striving for something better for the family. The man they'd called "Dad" hadn't cared enough to budge for anyone or anything.

Growing up, Blake remembered striving constantly to win the old man's approval, but no honors or awards or achievements ever worked. Trent had done the opposite—become a devil and a screw-up, as if driven to prove that he didn't give a damn if the old man noticed him or not. Now, it struck Blake's sense of irony that the twin brothers had actually been very much alike. They'd both been responding to the tense undercurrents in the house where they'd grown up.

And all that trouble had been caused by Larry Kincaid.

Blake thought he'd accepted all the new truths he'd discovered—until he'd met up with Serena and Nate. Finding out that he'd sired a son still stuck in his craw like a sore bear tooth. He'd never been irresponsible. He'd never been anything like his blood father, and he hated every association to the man. Even Remmington's wimpy coldness had been better than the kind of man who'd seduce a young woman and take off.

But now, looking at his brother, he hated the years the two brothers had wasted fighting like a snake and a mongoose. Maybe they were completely different. But Trent had had his world upturned, just like Blake. Their new problem wasn't alienation anymore, but just plain not knowing how to talk to each other.

"Hey..." Trent broke the silence first by motioning to the long, oblong package Blake was carrying. "I couldn't help but notice the toy bag. Don't tell me you're goofing off? Playing? You, the eternal workaholic?"

Months back, Blake would have taken offense at the tease, and likely come back with some comment about Trent's gambling, vagabond ways. Now he was too aware that they both had another chance at forging a family relationship, if at least one of them had the guts to take the first step. "No, I'm still working the same long hours. I wasn't shopping at the toy store for me."

"It looks like a game. I take it you've got a young friend."

"More like...a son."

"Pardon?" Trent was still grinning, cocking his head as if he were positive he'd misheard.

Blake had never planned to blurt it out, yet he didn't regret telling Trent. When push came to shove, no matter how often the two had bickered and fought, he trusted his brother. And if anything happened to him, Blake wanted someone to know that Nate was blood kin and for Trent to know that he had a nephew, as well. He lifted his hand in an unconscious and awkward gesture. "Hell, I never meant to bring this up in a chance conversation on the street. But I have to admit, there's about nothing else on my mind these days. I just found out recently that I had a son."

"How the hell could you—" Trent frowned, then clipped off whatever question he'd been about to ask. For two seconds the men's eyes met, sharing something they never had before. "It had to kill you to make a mistake. You were always pretty understanding when someone else screwed up, like me. But you could never tolerate it in yourself, no way, ever."

"It wasn't deliberate carelessness."

"Like you needed to tell me that. You all right with the situation?"

"Right now, no." Blake shifted on his feet. Okay, so he was glad he'd confided in Trent. But a man couldn't master Mount Everest on his first climb. These were heavy waters for two brothers who'd never talked. "I'm working on it. And to be honest, I don't know where anything's going right now, but I want you to know about your nephew. Another time maybe we could talk about it a little more. Just not now."

Trent nodded. "I'm late right now besides. Gina's parents are visiting, and I'm scheduled to do something with them, so I have to go." He hesitated. "And I heard you. You're not ready to give me all the details right now. But how about if we do something next week?"

It was Blake's turn to hesitate. "Yeah, I'd like that."

"We could just put our feet up, have a beer. Don't have to talk about anything heavy."

"Sounds good."

Even after Trent started walking away, Blake found himself staring at his brother's back. Trent used to be a devil, but he'd never been a happy devil. These days he had a smile bigger than the Montana sky. Gina had clearly made a giant difference in his life. He still had that live-for-today swagger, but it wasn't just a gambling bent that had turned him into a wildcatter back when. Trent had always lived on the edge, courted the rim of trouble. Now the toughness and mean edges all seemed gone.

Maybe Blake really could tell him more about the situation with Nate.

And maybe not.

Hustling, he hiked to his Acura, stashed the toy package, and wheeled out of Whitehorn toward Serena's place. Although it still wasn't raining, a fretful wind tumbled the prairie grasses, and overhead the clouds had darkened and were bunching in big fists. Blake could feel his pulse quicken, his stomach knot.

He still didn't understand exactly what had happened the other night. He'd started out feeling wronged, and somehow ended up feeling in the wrong—and still did. Serena should have told him about Nate, yes. But the real wrong in the situation had his name on it. The reality was that he'd failed her and Nate. No father had been in the picture when they'd both needed one.

No different than his real dad who had never been there for him or Trent.

Still, it was kissing her that had put the bow on his personal guilt package. He wasn't prepared for the titanium-sharp tug of hormones. But that was no excuse. He had no business touching her this time, any more than he'd had the right to make love with her on that long-ago night years before. Impulse had never been part of his character. He'd never given in to selfish needs.

Except with her.

Well, there was no reason to be afraid, Blake told himself as his fingers drummed an off-beat rhythm on the steering wheel. He wasn't afraid of Serena. Or of Nate. He needed to see this whole circumstance as an opportunity.

No kid had a choice in who fathered him, which Blake knew damn well. But Blake had a choice with his son—a choice to prove what kind of man he was, what kind of dad he could be, before Nate was stuck with the relationship. And Serena....

All right, all right. He'd never felt anything for any

other woman like he did for Serena. Then or now. But this was an opportunity to make that right, too. He'd be careful with her. Infinitely careful.

This time he'd do everything right. Or die trying.

Serena had never been a nervous person, which she reminded herself as she paced around the circular hearth in the living room. She glanced out the picture window. Again. Peered at the wall clock. Again. Chewed on a thumbnail. Again.

Abruptly she saw Blake's car pulling into her drive and charged for the door. This was so silly. All morning she'd had this foolish premonition that his visit was going to go all wrong. Naturally she was a little anxious, but she wasn't roiled up in a negative way. It was more like all her cylinders were firing with anticipation. She couldn't help remembering how much she'd once loved him. If she could have chosen someone to father her child, she'd always have chosen Blake.

Her feelings, of course, didn't matter. Her son was the only thing that mattered, but Serena had no real reason to worry that Nate wouldn't take to Blake. Nate accepted people. He was a happy kid, easygoing, content within himself. Maybe he was a little too mature for his age, but his extra dose of IQ undoubtedly came from Blake's genes—which gave them a common thread to relate with each other, right off the bat.

Blake had too much integrity to make a promise he wouldn't keep. He'd never rush something that wasn't right. So all that was happening this afternoon was Nate and Blake spending a little time together. Just being together. Nothing more. There was no reason on earth to have this odd premonition it was going to turn into an afternoon from hell.

As he got out of his car, he spotted her in the doorway. She saw his slow smile. All the blood dropped from her brain and pooled in a nice warm hormonal puddle just below her belly. Thirty-two years of maturity instantly flew out the door when she pushed it open, thinking, Come on, you dimwit. Get a grip.

She got a grip and smiled radiantly back. "You're early."

"Too early?"

"It's Saturday. No such thing as too early or too late, Doc. It's real-life time on the weekend. And what's that under your arm?"

"A little something I got for Nate. Just a game. I hope that's okay. I thought if I brought something we could do together, it might be easier for him to have a reason to talk to me."

"Bribery, you mean."

"No, no—"

At his sudden stricken look, Serena rolled her eyes. "Come on in and relax. I was teasing." Once he stepped inside, she meant to immediately fetch Nate, and yet for a moment she didn't move. "He's been playing something in the den this morning. I'll get him, but first…"

"What?"

He was standing right next to her, so close that she could see those mesmerizing blue eyes of his, feel the sun's heat coming off his skin, feel the electrical charge from kisses shared four days ago. Four long, long days ago. Stunning her like a slap was how fiercely and suddenly she wanted his mouth on hers again, could already imagine tasting him.

The only thing going seriously wrong with the afternoon so far, Serena thought ruefully, was her.

"First, I just want to be sure we're still in agreement about doing this low-key. Nate knows you were a friend from when we were both younger. That it's natural you'd stop by to say hi and catch up. Hang out for a few hours or whatever's comfortable. We'll show you around the place. Just take it easy."

"Sounded like a good plan to me when we talked about it. Still does."

And he still looked like the good man she'd first fallen like a rock for. The hair was fresh brushed, the chin fresh shaved. He wore tropic-weight khakis, sandals, a white T-shirt. Not true grubbies like normal people wore on a weekend, but probably as close to let-loose clothes as Blake owned.

There was nothing formal about the way he looked at her, though. His gaze shimmied down her length, checking her over as if they'd voted to play doctor and she was the patient. She was wearing an orange shirt and faded denim cutoffs, her hair braided and twisted up to get it off her neck in the heat—but she felt his gaze on her bare throat, her wrists, her long brown legs. Not sexual body parts. Just…regular body parts. But he made her feel as if she'd been touched. Intimately.

Still, Blake had barely stepped in the door before his expression changed. His gaze darted around the room and she saw hope in his eyes. Not for her, not about her, but about her son. Even though Serena'd told him that Nate was playing in the den, he was obviously hoping to catch a look at the boy. He didn't look much older than Nate right then. Worried, hoping, expectant, like a child waiting for a birthday party but not quite sure the plans were going to work out.

"Hey, it'll be fine, Blake," she said gently. "We're just going to have an easy couple of hours together. There's nothing to worry about. We'll have some serious things to decide later. But not today."

His eyes shot to hers again. "I know that." He sighed edgily. "And I promise I won't say or do anything that makes him uncomfortable, Serena."

"You wouldn't be here if I didn't trust you. Everything's going to be fine. Just make yourself at home, okay?" Swiftly she turned and headed down the hall. "Nate? Honey, we've got company."

"Oh, yeah? Who?" Nate's tousled head appeared from around the door of the den. He glanced around, noticed Blake—and promptly hightailed it to the bathroom faster than a gunned engine.

At the sound of the door slamming, Serena's mouth

dropped. "Nate?" Embarrassed, she shot a quick shrug at Blake. "I don't know what's going on here."

"Offhand, I'd say I seem to be the last person in the universe he's willing to see."

"No, no, he doesn't even know you. It can't be anything like that. And he knows his manners. Something must be wrong. I'll find out what the problem is. You sit down, okay? Put your feet up?"

Swiftly she jogged to the bathroom, rapped once on the door, then poked her head inside. Nate wasn't exactly in sight, but she noticed the small figure sitting in the bathtub with a gigantic turquoise towel over his head that didn't precisely conceal him as well as he'd planned—particularly since he'd tried that hiding trick on his mom before. In times of trouble, she'd climbed into the bathtub to talk with him.

"Hey, handsome," she said. "What's the problem here? Dr. Blake came over to say hi to both of us. How come you took off?"

From beneath the turquoise towel came a small voice. "Come on, Mom. You know why. He gave me a shot."

"But that was when you were sick."

"Yeah, well. He wants me to carry a shot around all the time. You heard him. He expects me to know how to poke myself with a needle."

"Sweetheart, you heard what he said. If you got stung by another bee, you could get sick really bad. The shot is to make you get better fast. Dr. Blake was treating you like a big boy, because he figured out that you were old enough to understand that nobody like shots, but sometimes that's what we have to do. So they're a pain. So what? They're still better than being seriously sick for a long time.''

Nate heard this out, and changed tactics—but no way that towel was coming off his head yet. ''Look, Mom. You let me make my own friends. You can make your own friends, too. But I'm not going near anybody who gives shots. No doctor friends for me.''

Serena poked her head under the towel to force a little eye-to-eye contact. ''I think that's being mean. And it isn't like you to be mean. He didn't come here to give you a shot. He just came here because we're old friends, and he wants to spend a little time with us. So this is about manners. When someone comes to the house, we come out and say hello and shake hands. You know that.''

''Mom—''

''We also don't decide whether we like somebody before we even know them—and you don't know Dr. Blake at all. What if someone decided they didn't like you because you have black hair? Wouldn't you think that was unfair?''

''I'd think they were stupid. But it's not the same. I just don't think it's a good idea to make a friend with someone who gives shots. Mom, you've told me a zillion million times that I should trust my feelings. Well, I trust that I hate grown-ups who give shots.''

Damn kid. Six years old and already turning her parental value lessons against her. She firmly pulled off the towel. "Come on, Nate. Think about it. You're holding it against Dr. Blake because he tried to help you. Now does that make sense? You know it doesn't. And worse yet, we're both being rude now. You don't have to like every grown-up who comes in the house, but I expect you to be polite. It's the Cheyenne way to always be respectful to those older than us."

Slowly Nate climbed out of the bathtub, but he sighed. His no-one-ever-suffered-like-me sigh. "Ice cream after dinner," he bargained.

"Okay."

"Fudge ripple."

"Okay."

"Two scoops."

"Okay." God, she was so ashamed. How come real parenting always came down to bribery? But somehow she had to con her monster-darling into giving Blake another chance. Nate was usually so tolerant and easygoing, but she should have anticipated that doctors weren't exactly the most popular people for urchins that age.

Back in the living room, Blake was standing at the window, jingling change in his pocket. He whirled around when he heard their footsteps, and his whole face lit up for his son. Serena felt a punch in her stomach she'd never expected. It was just that the yearning in Blake's eyes darn near tore her heart out.

"Hey, Nate," Blake said easily.

"Hey, Doc."

"You were busy playing something in the other room, huh? And your mom made you come out."

"Yeah, but it's okay." He shot out his small hand, as taught.

A muscle in Blake's cheek twitched as he gravely shook his son's hand, grown-up fashion. "It's okay if you'd rather go back to playing whatever you were doing. But I had this thing I'd like to give you first, if you wouldn't mind."

"Sure. Okay."

Blake leaned over and handed him the toy store bag, but then paused uncertainly. "I'd better tell you, I'm around kids all the time, but almost always when they're sick. It's not like I get a chance to play with them, so I really wasn't sure what kind of game might be up your alley."

Again, Serena felt her heart catch. It should have been Nate's eyes that looked hungry and hopeful at the idea of a present, but it was Blake who looked so nakedly yearning, so hoping to please. But then she saw the logo of the specific game when Nate pulled it out of the bag, and she had to swallow fast.

Most kids Nate's age loved that game but Nate had outgrown it a couple years before. Blake, of course, had no way of realizing that his son had charged way ahead of his age group and had already turned into a pint-size computer guru.

"Boy, is this cool. Thanks a lot," Nate said, and looked at her.

*You can have forty scoops of fudge ripple, you dar-*

*ling.* She didn't say it, but she sent him the message with her eyes, hoping that her favorite son in the entire universe would just understand how much she appreciated his being so tactful.

"It's all right? Really?" Blake asked.

"Yeah, really. It's a real nice game." Nate looked at her again.

*Sixty scoops.*

"I could play it with you. If you had the time," Blake offered carefully.

"Sure, Doc. I'd love to play it with you." Nate looked at her again.

*All right, you blackmailing devil. You can have a lifetime of fudge ripple. Just keep being nice.*

She crossed fingers behind her back as the two set up the game. She just wanted it to go well, for both their sakes. She wanted them to like each other, to find a way to relate to each other.

But somehow she'd never expected the heart-slug of emotion when she saw the two heads, so close, bent over the board game. Yes, she'd seen them together in the doctor's office, and that first shock of seeing Blake with his son had eclipsed her heart then, too. But this was way, way more heart-twisting. This was sitting on a couch together. Not in a sterile, professional doctor's office, but in a home—the way she'd never thought any of them could possibly be.

Suddenly Serena's smile died. She was painfully aware of all the risks they were gambling with. Her son, having to come to terms with a father in his life.

Blake, struggling with the knowledge that he was a father and what that meant to him.

And then there was her. Because Serena achingly realized that she was still in love with a man who didn't love her—and never had.

# Four

Serena was unsure how a short visit had turned into an all-day marathon, but somehow Blake was still here. Though she'd always considered washing dishes to be an insufferably tedious chore, tonight it was kind of fascinating. Everyone she knew washed dishes the same way—lifted a dish, rinsed or scrubbed off any loose food, then put the sucker in the dishwasher. Maybe it was boring, but anyone could do it. Even children. Even men.

But then there was Blake.

For the fourth time, he lifted a plate and just stood at her kitchen sink, holding it in midair.

If he didn't quit this behavior soon, Serena thought grimly, she was going to be forced to kiss him. Damn the man, but he had to stop doing endearing things or she just wasn't going to be responsible. He was the one who'd offered to do the dishes after being invited to their makeshift dinner of burgers on the grill. And that was fine. Except that every time he picked up a dish or glass, he stared out the kitchen window and completely forgot the washing job.

From where Serena stood next to him, she had the

same window view as Blake. Nate was outside, rolling in the grass, giggling that big-belly, infectious giggle only kids can do. It was that time of early evening when only children would willingly be outside. All breezes had died. The sun, which had earlier burned off the clouds, was still choking high. Even with the water garden happily bubbling, the heat was intensely smothering. Nothing was willingly moving. Nothing was willingly breathing, except for her son, who was watching Whiskey trying to nap at the same time the old setter was being stalked and hunted by the two kittens.

"Darn kid cheated. Actually cheated. So I'd win a game of Candyland, for God's sake," Blake muttered morosely. His gaze was glued on Nate as if all life would end if he missed a single breath the boy took.

"Yup, he did." Since he'd been holding the milk glass for a good sixty seconds without moving, Serena pried his fingers loose and deposited it in the dishwasher. Swiftly Blake picked up another plate, as if conscious he'd been slacking and was determined to now do double his share. Except that his gaze sneaked out the window again.

"And then I blew up his volcano." Blake's voice sounded bleak and guilt-ridden.

"I don't think we need to exactly call that a tragedy." Tactfully, slyly, she removed the plate from his hand. "It was just a vinegar and baking soda volcano, after all. We make them all the time. It's one of our favorite science experiments. The next time you'll know not to use quite so much baking soda.''

"That's not the point. It was the kid's volcano. The six-year-old kid's. And I'm the one who blew this stuff up all over your kitchen.'' The eyes turned to her were on fire with the depth of his anguish.

"Um, Blake, maybe we could lighten up? Nothing earth-shattering or life-threatening happened. Trust me. This kitchen has seen a few disasters before.'' By dancing around him—God knew, nothing was going to make the man budge from that window and get out of her way—she managed to scoop up the silverware and the last of the dishes. Two seconds later the dishwasher was slammed shut and switched on. Blake still hadn't moved. Then he looked at her, not seeing her, not seeing anything but failure spelled in capital letters.

"I did everything wrong I could possibly do. Even the squirt guns. I was so positive you'd be opposed to his having guns—''

Her jaw almost dropped in surprise. "Well, of course I am. But squirt guns are hardly the same thing as guns, Blake. I mean, what's a hot summer without a squirt gun? Naturally I have the biggest and the strongest squirter because I'm the mom.'' She thought she could woo a smile, but no.

"He hates me, Serena.''

"He does not.''

"He's never going to forgive me for giving him a

shot. And then the game I brought was all wrong. Stupid.''

''It's a good game for that age group. You had no way of knowing that Nate was beyond it. You're just getting to know him, for heaven's sake.''

''Yeah, well. After everything I screwed up, he'll never want to get to know me. He even tried to show me the computer game, that Wild Warriors? I killed off the hero in the first two minutes. I screwed up everything. Nate's going to hide if I try to visit again.''

She opened her mouth…and closed it. She wanted to say something reassuring, but the truth was, Blake had screwed everything up. Just as he'd said.

Any other time, the situation would be totally funny. Blake wasn't just good with kids. He was incredible. Even when he'd been a snot-nosed medical student, the older docs would call him in if they had an unhappy young patient, because Blake had such an unbeatably soothing way with children. But he'd walked in, seen Nate and froze. All afternoon, he'd been stiff as a rod. Artificial. Bumbling. Instead of just being himself, his conversations had been more formal than a zombie's.

She tried teasing, the way she had years ago when they were both in medical school—back then, her purpose in teasing was so he'd never guess how much she really cared. It worked then. All too well. ''Remmington, you're whining. Quit it.''

"Whining? Me?" He looked startled, as if such an accusation were unimaginable.

"Look," she said patiently, "we'll set up something else. Maybe the three of us could go fishing or kite flying, something like that. But next time, don't try so hard, for Pete's sake. Just relax. Loosen up. Be yourself."

"Relax," he echoed. "Loosen up…" He sounded as if he were gravely trying to memorize a set of instructions.

It was the last straw for Serena. She hurled the dish towel onto the turquoise counter and reached for him.

A hug was all she had in mind. Kisses had proved so volatile the other night that there was absolutely no chance she wanted to drive even near that ditch again. But a plain old ordinary hug was necessary. Blake was so miserable that she couldn't stand it, and she'd never seen him in such a disastrous state. Normally he had a terrific sense of humor and a natural sense of compassion. Even though he was being downright goofy about always doing the right thing, he still had a gift for making others feel comfortable around him. Yet with Nate, he'd been as comfortable to be with as a porcupine.

The circumstances were unsettling for him, Serena realized perfectly well. Nate was his son. Discovering so suddenly that he was a father was understandably traumatic. But what had drawn her to him years ago was sensing that Blake was afraid. Not of hard things. Not of danger, or insurmountable problems, or pain, or all the other serious things that everybody else in the universe was afraid of.

Blake was afraid of being human. Afraid of needing. That's what had driven her into his arms seven years ago, and damned if it didn't drive her just as crazy now. She charged forward, her arms swooping around his waist.

"Blake..." Her cheek nuzzled into his shoulder. "I want you to cut it out. You're being ridiculously hard on yourself. And, sure, this is an uncomfortable situation, but you're only making it worse. We'll tell him about your being his dad when it seems right to both of us. But it's not like this is a race. There's no deadline, no fire. For that matter, we don't need to know at this exact minute how you're going to fit in his life—or if you should—or how any of this is going to work out. I think some of those answers will show up if we just take it easy. Breathe. Let it be. Spend a little casual time together."

One minute, she was delivering that prosaically sensible lecture...and the next minute, the whole world went to hell.

One minute, her mouth was talking to his collarbone. The next, her lips were crushed under his. One minute, she was snuggled into an affectionate hug between old friends. The next, she was laid up against him like a flower connected to its life source.

One minute—one short minute ago—she'd been trying to communicate serious things to Blake. Important things. That he was a good man. That no matter how touchy or difficult the situation was, she trusted him. That she'd never doubted his integrity.

Her opinion hadn't exactly changed. It was just that from absolutely nowhere, in the middle of that nice ordinary hug, he'd suddenly cocked his knuckles under her chin. The instant her face tilted, his mouth pounced on hers, prowled hers, took hers faster than a bank robber in a getaway car.

The tile floor in her kitchen was suddenly shaking, which was pretty amazing considering this part of Montana had never suffered an earthquake. Worse yet, she remembered this feeling. In seven years she hadn't felt it. In seven years, she hadn't wanted it.

It was frightening to discover a need this huge—but the sensation was exactly how it had been between them before. Hunger like an explosion. Desire like a fire. A need that seemed to surge from a desperate loneliness. Blake always had people around him, yet he'd always kept himself so self-contained. There was only one other time he'd allowed that private door to peek open—at least around her—and the result had been like a blast furnace blowing out, blowing up, out of both their controls.

Lips whispered over lips, bit, then whispered again. His first kiss was tender-rough. That one fed into another, coaxed into another, seeped into a haunting fourth kiss that involved tongues and tastes. Her mind was spinning at the luring taste of him, the promise, the sensation of being captured and captivated. She felt his hard muscular chest against her breasts, the heat shimming off his skin—not because the early evening was hotter than a cyclone, but because of her. Because he was hot for her. And Blake, that other time, had ripped all her moral and sensible moorings loose because of the naked, wicked longing he'd communicated to her. It was as if he'd never loved until he touched her.

More tantalizing yet—more terrifying yet—she felt exactly the same way.

A screen door suddenly slammed. "Hey, Mom. Hey, Dr. Blake." One hand showed up on the other side of the kitchen counter. The lid on the ceramic cookie jar clattered open. The small, grubby hand filched two Oreos, replaced the jar lid and disappeared from sight again. Footsteps pattered down the hall, trailed by the clicks and claws of his critter sidekicks.

Still, it was Blake's sharp hands on her shoulders that forced Serena's eyes open. She didn't want to wake from this misty dream. Her body hadn't felt charged this way in so long. It wasn't just the joyful, exciting lustiness but the feeling of being five hundred percent alive and female, the way she'd never been with anyone else. If this wasn't wise, she didn't care. In her heart, in her head, Serena believed in the court of emotions. Nothing could be wrong that felt this right. So there were risks. So there were problems. Even terrible, frightening problems.

But she loved those kisses. And she loved being kissed by Blake.

Slowly, though, her heartbeat simmered down and

then stilled. Blake's hands dropped, as if burned by her shoulders. Guilt flamed in his eyes. He swallowed hard.

"Serena. Did he see us?"

"I don't know." Her voice was still breathless. His fault.

"My God. I swore I wouldn't make anything about this tough for Nate. Or you. That I'd be careful. I'm sorry—"

"I'm a grown woman. I could have stopped you if I'd minded being kissed."

"That doesn't make it right."

Her eyes searched his. She wanted to see the light in his face that had been there moments before, the light that had been there for her, in the moments when nothing else existed but the two of them. Instead she saw the responsible frown, the worry in his gaze. The good-man-Blake...but the Blake who had never really seen her. Years before or now. "I don't think kissing right now was the most sensible idea we've ever had. I'll grant you that much. But as far as I know, the civilized world as we know it wasn't completely annihilated because we lost our heads for a couple of seconds."

"You're making a joke. But I don't think it'll seem so funny if Nate saw us and starts asking questions."

"Blake—"

"What?"

"Go home," she ordered him.

* * *

Blake prowled restlessly around his kitchen. *Go home,* she'd told him. Well, he'd been home for an hour and the truth was, he figured he was lucky Serena hadn't skinned him alive before kicking him out.

Irritably he opened a cupboard, spotted bottles of brandy and whiskey, slammed it. He'd never been a big drinker, but since discovering his real father had died with a bourbon in one hand and a cigar in the other, somehow he'd lost all taste for even a shot of hard liquor. Right then, though, he needed something. He yanked open the refrigerator, saw grapefruit juice and pop and a carton of milk. Yanking out the carton, he took a long pull.

It didn't help. Serena's face stole into his mind and filled up all the empty spaces.

He took a second long gulp, then slammed the refrigerator door closed and, hands on hips, paced a new hole in the ash-gray carpet in the living room. Blinds dulled the light, concealed the vibrant colors of sunset. The rental house on Stoney Ridge Road was a short mile from his pediatrician's office and that was all he'd cared about when he'd come back to Whitehorn. A place to hang his hat that was convenient to his work. He didn't really live here. When it came down to it, he didn't really live anywhere.

Blake paced from window to door, then from door back to window. The one thing he'd always done right in his life was behave like a decent man. Except, of course, with Serena. So far he was batting zero with her. He'd done everything wrong he could possibly do. He'd gotten her pregnant and disappeared from her life without even asking if that one night had consequences. Yes, damn it, she should have told him, but he'd known for quite a few years that it took two to tango, so it was up to him to make sure he did the responsible, honorable thing. So fine—a little late—he finally shows up years later, only to bumble into her life like a case of poison ivy.

She didn't want him, didn't need him. That was obvious after the first meeting. It was equally obvious to Blake that she'd have found a reason or a way to tell him about Nate *if* she believed he'd be a decent father. So, Blake figured, he'd have to prove he was worthy of being a dad. No sweat. He didn't want to risk being in Nate's life unless he could prove that to himself and to Nate, as well as Serena.

He pounded a fist into his palm. He'd sure shown her, hadn't he? And his son. One day with Nate and all he'd done was bore the kid witless. The kid was six years old and already had nice, polite manners and tact. But hell, Blake never imagined that his own son would have to practice tact on him. Then there was the business of jumping Serena. Right in the kitchen. Right in the window. Right where his son could have seen them—had walked in on them, for that matter. He never jumped women. Ever.

Just twice in his life.

And both times it was the same woman.

He stormed back into the kitchen to take another wallowing gulp from the milk carton. The real irony

was that being a decent guy had never been that hard
a challenge. It was just when he got near Serena that
every good-man thought flew out of his head. He
couldn't explain it. She was a woman who giggled at
sunshine and sang when she drove. A woman who
seemed to find joy even in the corners of a dark day.
She was light and exuberant life and as naturally sensual as a dew-dripping rose, a good person from the
inside out. So there was no understanding why his
fantasies of her were all wicked. All wild. All amoral.

He heard an abrupt knock on his front door and
swiftly ran for it. God knew, he was expecting no one
at nine on a Saturday summer night, but he was so
grateful for the interruption that he didn't care who it
was.

Just as he reached the door, Garrett Kincaid turned
the knob and cocked his head inside. "It's perfectly
okay if you kick me out. I should have called before
coming. I never like dropping by without warning,
but I was already in town and I just wondered how
you were getting on."

"Just fine, sir. And I'm glad you stopped by. Come
on in." Automatically, Blake extended a courteous
hand, then ushered the older man toward the chairs
in the living room. Mentally he wanted to kick himself for calling him sir. Garrett had never treated him
formally, in fact he'd warmly encouraged Blake to
call him "Grandfather." But the relationship was still
so new that it was hard for Blake to feel comfortable

with it, even though he'd both liked and respected Garrett Kincaid from their first meeting.

This evening, as before, Garrett's ramrod-straight posture denied his seventy-two years. His straight hair had gone silver, but his features were strong, his eyes kind as they first studied his grandson, then wandered around the room. "Neat as a pin. Just like it was last time. Of course, you haven't added a single thing to gather dust."

"Um, I'm not much on collecting doodads and decorating. What can I get you to drink?"

Garrett slapped down his Stetson, then settled slowly in a dove-gray chair under a window. "Willow bark tea, if you've got it."

"Somehow I sense I'm being teased," Blake said dryly.

"Because you are. No common sense natural remedies for a high-class Los Angeles doctor, huh?"

"Ex-L.A. doctor. And I may not have willow bark, but now that I'm a high-class Montana doctor, I can probably scare up some ibuprofen for you. You want it with water, iced tea? Are we talking arthritis?"

"We're talking a man who's too old to spend seven hours on a horse in heat like today. But I never could stand being idle, so I'm just stuck paying the price. And water will do. But I didn't come here to talk about my aches and pains." Again Garrett's gaze swept the room, taking only a second to visually vacuum the contents. "I'd hoped you'd be more settled in by now."

"I am settled." The instant Blake fetched the ice water and tablets, he tried to subtly examine his grandfather's coloring and general health without getting his head bitten off. Though whipped, Garrett looked fine. He was as straightforward and perceptive as in their first meeting.

"No. You're just camping here still. No pictures on the wall. No color. Nothing of your own. I'd hoped once you spent a little time in Whitehorn that you'd want to stay."

"To be honest, I haven't made any long-term plans. For right now I'm happy to be back in White-horn, happy to get to know you, and I couldn't feel luckier at Carey needing another pediatrician. I love the kids, the office setup, everything about joining her practice. So far, people seem to have accepted me back with no problems. If anything, they've been un-expectedly welcoming." Except for the only two peo-ple who really mattered to him. But his grandfather was the last person with whom Blake would willingly discuss Serena and Nate.

"Did you think the townspeople wouldn't be wel-coming?" Garrett studied him again, then sighed. "You're still troubled. You thought folks would judge you because of who your father was? And are you feeling shamed to find out whose blood is in your veins?"

Blake met his eyes. "I won't lie and say your son was someone I'd ever emulate. But I was both honored and proud to find out that you were my grandfather, sir.''

"Hell. You've got better manners than I do. You're also a kinder man.'' Garrett leaned forward. "But I just had a feeling we needed to talk about this a little more. In my opinion, the only shame in this situation is mine. You had no choice in who sired you. I had choices about how I raised my son. Somehow I failed to raise Larry with honor and principles.''

"No.'' From the start, Blake had felt drawn to the older man's sense of justice. "Blaming yourself isn't right. Maybe if a child goes through some terrible tragedy, they've got an excuse for turning out rough. Otherwise, when a man grows up, it's up to him to quit hiding behind excuses and to take control of his own life. My father had no business stepping out on his wife, much less populating the country with a half dozen illegitimate kids.''

Just saying the words stabbed Blake's conscience with a guilt-sharp knife. He had, of course, produced an illegitimate son of his own. That his father's blood flowed in his veins nagged like a sore on his soul. He'd never meant to be careless with Serena. He'd never knowingly desert a woman in trouble, or a child. Yet he'd done both things—just like his scoundrel of a father.

"Blake,'' Garrett said quietly, "something is seriously bothering you.''

"No, I'm fine.''

"Have you talked to your father since you found

out about your Kincaid background—obviously, I
mean the father who raised you, Harold Remmington?''

"No. Neither has Trent. But we've both been es-
tranged from him since my mother died. There was
no sudden hostility, but none of us ever had a family
feeling. Now, of course, I know why. He knew he
wasn't our father.'' Blake stood and ambled toward
the window to flick open the blinds. Nothing outside
to see; night was dropping faster than a stone. But
weeks before he'd realized that Garrett hated feeling
cooped up and started acting antsy and claustrophobic
if he couldn't see outside. "If Harold called, I'd help
him if I knew he needed something. But after Mom
died, he moved, retired south. He's made no effort to
keep in touch with me or Trent.''

"So you have no one in your life from before,''
Garrett said thoughtfully.

From before it was discovered that Larry Kincaid
was his real father, Blake understood him to mean.
"If you're asking if I have anyone to count on, I don't
need anyone. For that matter, if there was some crisis,
I have a brother. And you've been nothing but real
family to me from the day we met. There's no problem, sir.''

"I didn't encourage you to come back to Whitehorn to make you unhappy.''

"I wanted to come back. To meet you, spend time
with you. And once I was divorced...well, I'd become disillusioned with big-city doctoring by then,

anyway. I don't know that I'll stay. I don't know where I belong, if you want to know the truth. But the last thing you need to do is worry about me, sir."

"I'd just hoped…" Garrett hesitated. "I'd never have known about my son's behavior if he hadn't developed a conscience at the end and left a letter in his will. But by contacting you and the others, I'd hoped to make things right. Not just by leaving you a slice of the Kincaid ranch, but by being kin to you."

"I understand about that drive to make things right. I think you passed that trait straight on to me," Blake said with a touch of humor. "I never could sit still more than two seconds when I felt responsible and capable of making something better."

"Blake?"

"What?"

"I'm proud you're my grandson. I'm just sorry I never had the chance to be your grandfather through your growing-up years." Garrett pushed at his knees, then stood up, carefully rolling his shoulders as if to shake out the kinks. "Would you come to dinner at the ranch on Sunday?"

"It seems to me I owe you an invitation the other way. But I'm not much on cooking, eating most of my dinners at the Hip Hop Café in town."

"Sounds fine by me. What day?"

Wily old man. A few minutes later Blake walked him to his pickup, thinking Garrett was one brilliant, manipulative dude. Blunt as bananas, but straightforward and honest. He wanted a relationship with his grandson—and all the other grandsons that his womanizing, philandering son-of-a-seadog Larry had fathered. But Garrett was nothing like his son. He was a good man. A moral man. With heart.

He'd been reaching out to Blake steadily for three months now.

Standing in the driveway, he watched Garrett's truck pull away. The sky had turned a dark sapphire. Lamplights were popping on in the neighborhood, screen doors clapping as moms called for their kids to come in, fireflies dancing in the front yards. An occasional car passed, but Whitehorn closed down early. Families were all gathered up by this time of night. There were still sounds—an occasional burst of laughter or screeches of rock and roll through the open windows, a dog barking, a baby crying.

Blake closed his eyes, inhaling all the smells and sounds of Whitehorn. It was home. But he wasn't sure now—any more than he'd been sure as a child—if he really belonged here.

But the image of a dark-eyed boy filled his mind. And then a dark-eyed, dark-haired woman with a smile that could rip a man's safe moorings to flotsam in two seconds flat. A man could believe in anything when Serena smiled a certain way.

A man could do anything when Serena kissed him a certain way.

He opened his eyes and swiftly pivoted toward the house. Maybe the longing had a chance of becoming real this time. Maybe, for the first time in his life, he

could feel as though he belonged somewhere, to
someone. But there was a catch to that hope, he knew.
He had to make things right—for Nate, for Serena.
He had to prove that he could be a good father, the
kind of father Nate would choose.

Even more, he wanted to be the kind of man Serena
would choose to be with. Not from obligation or because a child tied them in a relationship. But because
she wanted to be.

# Five

Putting Nate to bed always took wheedling, cajoling, and a little conniving. Her son loved every moment of being awake. He hated to waste a second of life doing anything as boring as sleeping. Eventually, though, the layers of play grime were soaked off, the computer unplugged, the cup of milk downed and the teeth brushed. Coaxing him under the covers wasn't hard at this point, but getting him to stop talking was.

"Can I go fishing tomorrow with Uncle Wolf and Uncle John?"

"After my brothers brought you home so sunburned you could hardly move last time? I don't think so. Your uncles are still in big trouble with me."

She pulled up the sheets, tucked just so. Whiskey attempted to slink onto the foot of the bed as if the two humans might accidentally miss noticing something the size of an Irish setter.

"Mom, you shouldn't be mad at them. We just got busy fishing and doing guy stuff. Important things." Nate already knew how to tease and get a rise out of her. His eyes twinkled.

"Important guy things like forgetting to show any common sense?"

"Yeah. Like that." Nate's hand slipped outside the covers and reached down to the floor. Seconds later a small, purring lump showed up under the sheet next to Nate's tummy. Both humans pretended not to notice that, too. "So, can I go fishing? Think about it. I'd be out of your hair for hours."

"I'm afraid that argument isn't worth beans. I happen to love you in my hair, short stuff." She bent down to nuzzle a forehead-to-forehead kiss—the kind that her big-boy son didn't mind so much because, in his words, it wasn't so smooshy. From the corner of her eye she caught George and the kittens in the doorway. "No. Scoot! There's no room for Nate in his own bed now."

"Aw, Mom. I like everybody to sleep with me. And even if you make 'em go away, they'll just come in later anyway."

"Uh-huh. But this way we can pretend that the humans of the house are in control." She scooped up a sock that had failed to make it to the hamper, turned off the overhead light, then sank back next to him on the bed. She made her voice sound as casual as a light spring breeze. "So, what'd you think of Dr. Blake coming over and spending some time with us?"

"I dunno. I guess it was okay. Once I could see for sure that he wasn't gonna try and give me any more shots."

"Hey, didn't I tell you that this wasn't about doctoring? That he just wanted to visit?" Serena ruffled his hair. "Besides, I just wanted to know what you thought of him."

"He was weird."

"Oh?" Serena mentally told herself not to worry too fast. "Weird" wasn't automatically a kiss-of-death opinion coming from a six-year-old. "Weird-bad or weird-funny or weird-cool?"

"Weird-kinda-interesting. At first I thought it was pretty dumb that he wanted to play a game with me. Because it was such a stupid game, you know?"

"Uh-huh."

"But then I figured, okay, he's a grown-up, and you never know what they're going to do." Nate heaved a world-weary sigh. "After that, though…well, I thought he'd be more fun when we were making volcanoes."

"I thought you two were having fun, then. I could hear you laughing in the kitchen."

"Well, yeah, we were. Until he got all upset because he made his wrong and the volcano bubbled all over the place and made a big mess. I told him you wouldn't be mad. I told him you'd even come help us clean it up if we couldn't do it ourselves, that we just had to try our best. We cleaned it up good, but it's like he was scared to play after that. Anyway. You can have him over again, Mom."

"It's okay if he comes over again? Even if you didn't have that good a time?" A velvet paw sneaked out from under the covers to attack her hand. Momentarily, though, her eyes were on her son.

"Yeah, it's okay. Because you know what I thought?"

"No, what?"

"That he's sad. And he's lonesome. 'Course, mebbe if he'd quit giving shots to kids all day, it'd be easier for him to make friends, you know? So you can have him around. We could play with him some more. Get him laughing and stuff. You know, like you and me. Then maybe he wouldn't be so sad and he'd get the idea how to play."

"That sounds like a plan." Serena stood, intending to leave for real this time, as soon as she gave him one more hug and buss. Then a snuggle. Then one last tuck. "Hey, did I mention to you recently that I think you're a pretty fabulous kid?"

"Cut it out, Mom. You're 'barrassing me. I hate that."

"I'm so sorry. I love you. Sometimes this stuff just slips out."

"Sometimes on purpose." Nate's eyes shifted to half-mast. "Anyway, he can come over, but I don't think you should kiss him again."

"Pardon me?" Serena was already at the door when her son's offhand comment made her stop dead.

"I don't think you and him should kiss anymore," Nate repeated clearly. "I can kiss you. You're my mom. But I don't like it when other guys kiss you, okay?"

"What's this? You've seen Uncle Wolf and Uncle John kiss me a hundred thousand million times."

"Not like *he* kissed you, Mom." Her son's soprano voice expressed an extremely sure opinion. Then he yawned and turned over.

Nate no longer seemed worried about kisses or anything else. Yet as Serena tiptoed down the hall to her bedroom, her mind replayed everything her son had said about Blake. Somehow Nate had picked up on the chemistry between her and Blake, and on his daddy's loneliness. But the answers she'd hoped to gain from their day together didn't seem clear. What did her son need? And what did Blake need? Was there any chance of their all relating as a family? How could she help the two males create a relationship together?

She switched on the table lamp in her bedroom, aware that all this fretful worrying was unlike her. The old sapphire prospectors used to say that you had to be willing to blow something up if you wanted to expose the jewels. She'd always secretly thought that was good life advice, too. Everything worthwhile took risk. If you wanted something big, then you had to be willing to take a big risk. Serena had never been afraid of stepping up and embracing life.

She'd taken a huge risk with her heart, once upon a time. She'd made love with Blake, knowing he was wrong for her.

She'd fallen in love with him all over again today, watching him struggle so hard with his son. And she realized achingly hard all over again that he was still wrong for her.

As she stripped off the day's clothes, she glanced around her bedroom with sober eyes. Nate called it her "treasure room." Glass doors led to an outside deck, where she was likely to sleep on a hot summer night such as this. The far corner held a small kiva fireplace and a hearth she'd laid herself in Italian tile. A Danish silver brush and mirror sat on her dresser. The dresser mirror was Samoan. Tribal masks hung on the far wall in teak and soft, rich zebrawood. The focus of the room, though, was the giant Chinese marriage bed—not a real one; she couldn't afford that. But she'd been charmed by the design in a museum and come home to make her own version, working with wood and silk hangings to duplicate the sense of an intimately enclosed, private sleeping space.

She pulled the band free from her long braid and shook her hair loose, grabbing the silver brush. However eclectic and goofy her decorating style, she loved the room. It represented exactly who she was. Unfortunately it also represented the stark differences between her and Blake.

Being born Cheyenne and raised by a white family, Serena figured that a woman belonged where she made a place for herself, her own way. She wanted to instill those same values in her son. She'd always believed that it made no sense to judge others by race or culture or differences, but that the adventure of life and people and all the differences were there to be embraced.

That was one of the frightening challenges she'd discovered when she first fell in love with Blake. She saw love as an adventure, a risk, a wonder. Blake saw love as a responsibility. She'd savored every perilous, precious sensation of loving him. He had only let loose that one time with her, and only then because he'd been so deeply in grief that he'd lost control. Otherwise, he never colored outside the lines, while she lived to do just that.

He was a man of honor, which she deeply respected. Then and now. But they might as well have been from different worlds. Then and now.

When the phone suddenly jangled by her bed, she was so deep in thought that she jumped, but the interruption was welcomed. Thinking about kisses—even soul-touching kisses—was dangerous. Thinking about the yearning and loneliness she'd seen in Blake's deep blue eyes was even worse. If she'd never met him again, maybe it wouldn't have mattered. But now she had. Now she could feel a chance. A chance to be with him again, a chance to make it together as a family. A chance—just one more shot— at showing him the wonder and adventure of love. Of life. Of the kind of life she'd once dreamed of sharing with him.

But he was as closed-up as he'd always been. She doubted he'd even really looked at her. He was only looking at her and Nate as a responsibility he was trying to make right. Damn. She had to get those hopes out of her mind. When the phone jangled a second time, she leaped to answer it, not just in fear the noise would wake Nate but to force her mind off Nate's dad completely.

"Serena? Oh, I'm so glad I reached you. This is Victoria—Victoria Rutherford."

She dropped her hairbrush in surprise. "Vic, I can hardly believe it's you! How terrific to hear from you. What's new? How are you doing?"

Although it had been years since they'd taken teaching courses together, Serena instantly pictured her old friend. Victoria was petite and blond and gorgeous, with big blue eyes and an elegant sense of style—Serena's opposite in every possible way. But the differences between them had never mattered, and neither had Victoria's choosing to teach a zillion miles away in some fancy east coast school. They'd always been able to pick up the friendship and talk as if they'd just seen each other yesterday.

"Well, I'm fine. Sort of."

"What's wrong?" Serena's easy smile immediately died.

"I'm coming home."

"That's wonderful!"

"Well, not exactly." Serena could suddenly hear the tears in her old friend's voice. "I'm coming home because I know my family's in financial trouble. The ranch has to be sold."

"Oh, I'm so sorry, sweetie."

"Thank you. And actually…nothing's that new about this. My dad's had trouble with his health. And I knew Mom and Dad were struggling. I just didn't realize they were this close to losing the ranch, so fast. If anything else happened, they didn't tell me. Anyway, I didn't mean to dump on you—"

"Cut it out," Serena chided her gently. "You know we're friends. You can dump on me any time. I'm just sorry you and your family are going through such a hard stretch. And when are you coming home? I realize you'll probably have your hands full, but maybe we can get together…or if there's anything I can do to help, just let me know."

They chatted awhile longer. Typically, even though Victoria had serious problems in her life, she didn't neglect to ask about Serena's.

"Blake Remmington has moved to Whitehorn, at least temporarily," Serena confessed.

"Blake? Really? The guy you told me about from years ago?"

"I had a feeling you'd remember. And if you're coming back home, I thought I'd better mention it so you won't be surprised if you see the name, or meet him."

So typically, Victoria cut to the chase. "Something's happening between you two, isn't it? He was always unfinished business for you."

"No, he wasn't."

"Oh, yeah he was." Victoria's voice was teasing, but then she let it go.

Eventually they both ended the conversation, but even after Serena hung up, her mind repeated her friend's intuition. Blake *was* unfinished business for her.

And there was something happening between them. After seeing him only a few times, and even under a terribly stressful situation, every feeling she'd ever had for him seemed to have grown tenfold.

He'd needed her before. And she sensed that he needed her now—or someone. Someone who could open the man up, teach him to embrace love and life and not worry so much about doing the right thing that he closed his life to the possibilities. But whether that someone could be her, Serena was no more sure now than she'd been seven years ago.

Humming rock and roll under her breath, Serena juggled a half dozen shopping bags as she ambled down Center Avenue. She never shopped, except for the obvious type of grocery and chore shopping. But her brothers had absconded with Nate for a fishing outing, which left her with a rare, whole day to waste. And she had. Her hair had a fresh cut and her nails a manicure, thanks to Kim, Gracie's daughter, at the Whitehorn Beauty Salon. The pockets of her white shorts had spearmint candy, her favorite, and her arms were filled with loot—the sponge cake that had leaped into her hands at the bakery, the two hot romances that had called to her at the bookstore, the turquoise sandals that walked into her bag at the shoe shop.

Of course, she was now starving and still in town and it was hotter than blazes, but she could both nap and eat once she got home. Wasting an entire afternoon was an accomplishment worth gloating over. No laundry, no picking up a single toy. She paused at the movie theater to check the marquee, then started to cross Center Avenue when she suddenly heard the blaring horn of a semitrailer.

The sun screamed in her eyes when she whirled around. It was that predinner sun, the hottest and brightest of the day. Even sun-blinded, though, she easily saw the purple semi cab, the driver way up there, laying on his horn as if he were trying to wake the dead and everyone in Whitehorn. She saw the truck. Saw the small red ball. Saw the little girl skipping after the ball.

In the next split second, Serena saw the truck try to, start to, want to, swerve, and the sick, frantic look on the driver's face through the dusty windshield.

Serena dropped her bags and charged for the child, even knowing she couldn't possibly reach her in time. She heard a woman's frantic shriek—it had to be the little girl's mom—but in the same instant, she saw Blake. He was already in the road, barreling at race-car speed right in the path of the semi. Within a blink of a second, he swooped up the little girl and hurled them both toward the sidewalk.

It was all over so fast. Serena grabbed her bags and the squished sponge cake, but kept moving, her gaze peeled on the scene.

Pedestrians and onlookers had run to the spot, but Serena could still see that Blake had crashed on the cement sidewalk with the child on top of him. By the time she reached them, the frizzy-blond mama was holding her frizzy-blond daughter and crying and trying to kiss Blake all at the same time.

The little girl appeared absolutely fine. The mom appeared as if she would recover, given some time. Only Blake seemed to be in any trouble, with a scrape on his hand and a tear on the right side of his khakis. The mom kept kissing him, and then the little girl started doing her share.

"I love you, Dr. Blake! You're my hero forever and ever!"

"I don't know how to thank you. Oh, my God! Oh, my God, I was so scared!"

Serena saw Blake tactfully try to extricate himself from his worshipers, but the onlookers were getting as big a charge from the scene as she was. Unfortunately, though, no one else was even trying to save him, which meant she obviously had to step in.

"Serena!" He didn't really need her hand to get himself up, or to handle his thankful admirers. But the moment their fingers twined, she felt the connection. Heat that had nothing to do with a sweltering August afternoon. Yearning that had nothing to do with Blake's desire to get out of a public situation. Intimacy that shouldn't have anything to do with the simple touching of two hands.

He eased to his feet, still talking to the mom and

daughter, his face flushed, his hand locked with Serena's as if their palms were glued together. Finally the mom took her little girl off, yelling about never running into the road for a ball or a toy again.

"Let's see the hand," Serena ordered.

"It's fine."

"I'm figuring you're lucky you didn't break it. It looked like you fell right on that hand, with all your weight and the little girl's, too. Now let's see."

"It's fine."

"Hey, you're not talking to a doc, Doc. You're talking to a mom. You either obey or die. That's the sum total of your choices."

Chuckling, he turned his left palm over. As she inspected the streaks of gravel, scraped skin and blood, she felt his gaze on her face, roaming her features as if he had nothing better to do than stare at her all day.

"Where's your sidekick?" he asked.

"Fishing with his two uncles. They won't be back until dark, so I had the whole day free. We're going into the Hip Hop Café," she informed him.

"You're hungry?"

"Yes, actually. But the point is, that's the closest bathroom and you know they'll have a first-aid kit there in the restaurant."

They did. Once they reached the Hip Hop, Serena hadn't exactly meant to stay with him, but somehow she ended up squeezed into a booth between his hip and the wall. Elvis was begging someone to love him tender on the old jukebox and, being Tuesday night, naturally the special was elk hash. Scents of a fresh apple cobbler and a still hot blueberry pie wafted through the air. Ceiling fans stirred the heat.

Janie Carson Austin managed the place, and maybe she was a penny pincher to have no air-conditioning, but she was a pro at customer-pampering in other ways. Seconds after she spotted Blake and Serena wandering in, she had Blake stashed in the front booth with the first-aid kit on the table between them. She went off to get them lunch, which she said was on the house for the town hero.

The Hip Hop was crowded. In the back retired sheriff Judd Hensley and his wife Tracy were visiting town and holding court, regaling the regulars with tales of their newly opened fishing camp. Deputy Clint Calloway was at the front counter, soaking in a coffee, being kidded by anyone who passed as to whether he'd managed to get his wife Dakota pregnant again. Emma Stover, the new waitress with the sweet face and the shy smile, was running a hundred miles an hour between tables. Then in walked Lily Mae Wheeler, the town gossip. She cast a narrowed eye at Blake and Serena who were seated in "her" booth, then wandered over to shake Blake's good hand. "Nice going, Doc, saving that little girl."

Before Blake could reply, Lily Mae sat across from him in the booth and, seemingly without breathing, regaled them with the latest gossip. "You know the Montgomerys, don't you? I never liked it, the way

Ellis never had a kind word for his daughter, and Christina such a darling—or at least she was until her mother died and she started running wild. Wild because she was lonely, I say. Only the point is now that she's missing. Everyone's talking about it. The whole world could see that tummy of hers growing big, no matter how much Christina denied being pregnant, but the real question is who on earth the father could be. And if she disappeared now because she ran off with the daddy of her baby. Now I hear Rachel Montgomery's coming home—that's Christina's oldest sister, if you didn't know—and for myself, I figure Rachel can get to the bottom of this if anyone can. She won't let it rest until we all know for sure what's happened to Christina.''

Homer Gilmore ambled past, poking his teeth with a toothpick, looking as glaze-eyed as ever, talking to himself. He usually came into the Hip Hop for the elk hash special and a chance to tell anyone who'd listen about the latest alien sighting. No one really knew what to do about Homer. The old man eked out a hand-to-mouth living in mining and he wasn't so goofy that he needed to be hospitalized, but his stories were definitely a walk on the wild side. Today was no different.

He stopped at the booth, his wizened face flushed, and delivered a convoluted, grizzy tale about an alien he'd come across near the sapphire mines. ''You know the place. The virgin woods, west from the reservation, where them ol' mines be. Still some good sapphires there.''

"Yes, Homer," Lily Mae said impatiently. Clearly she didn't want to be interrupted in her conversation with Blake.

"Well, it was rainin' two nights ago," Homer continued. "Rainin' so hard, I couldn't a seen nothin', 'cept that alien. Had a big ol' ray gun and no hair and crazy eyes. Didn't look like no kind of human, I tell ya."

"Yes, Homer."

"I weren't doin' nothin'. Just lookin' around fer them sapphires, y'know? Them stones can really shine right after a rain. But b'lieve me, it had no reason to attack me. That there alien were doin' somethin'. Bent over somethin'. A body, I think. Maybe tryin' to get it back to them there ship. When it seen me, it come at me with that ray gun. I run. Yes, sir, you cain't b'lieve how fast I run."

"Yes, Homer."

"Alien eyes, it had. Wild. Evil. No human look nothin' like them eyes. I figure it be the sapphires that calls to them aliens. Some kind of kinetic power in the stones that aliens can see from millions a' light-years away. But I cain't figure why it tried to git me. I weren't doin' no harm to nobody."

"Yes, Homer," Lily Mae said in a monotone voice. "You go home now. You can tell us some more about those aliens tomorrow." She gave him a little nudge to rather gently but firmly send him on his way. When Homer finally ambled on, still muttering about his newest alien encounter, Lily Mae turned back to Blake's injured hand—after sharing a commiserating smile at both of them. Homer was the town trial and most folks tried to be patient.

But right now there was simply important gossip to share. ''Serena, I swear you look more beautiful every time I see you. Is that a new haircut? I'll bet Kim cut your hair, didn't she? She's twice the stylist her mama ever was. How long she visiting for this time? Blake, you stay sitting still now. You need this here first aid. Now, where was I? Was I telling you about the Montgomery girl's disappearance or Jordan Baxter's feud with the Kincaids?''

''I swear, I'm fine,'' Blake said for the dozenth time.

''Nonsense. You're a man. You never know when you're fine, and none of you would clean a cut proper if left to your own devices. And you haven't said a word how you're doing in your practice with Carey. Everybody loves you, that's all I hear, but you've been home how long now? And you're still not talking. Everybody was asking earlier about the Hillerman boy's broken arm last week, and was it an accident or did that varmint father hurt him deliberately? You can tell me the real truth. I swear, I won't tell a soul!''

A half hour later, Serena and Blake spilled out the front door, both their stomachs filled with dinner and a double dessert—on the house. Blake's hand was bandaged as if it'd been broken in ten places instead of being slightly abraded, and he was shaking his head. "I've been eating there quite a bit, since coming back to town—anything's better than cooking on my own. But don't you ever feel like you've been through a war after spending a half hour there?"

Serena laughed. "The Hip Hop Café is a town institution, you know that. On the other hand, you can find out anything you want to know about anyone in there. It's cheaper than buying a newspaper."

"But it's so exhausting. I may have to break down and learn to cook, just to have a peaceful meal."

"Not that. Not a fate worse than death like cooking. Nothing's worth going that far."

Amused, Blake grabbed her arm. "You're right. Even surviving all that gossip is easier than having to do dishes. Do you have a few minutes?"

"A few minutes for what?"

"You said Nate was with your brothers so I was asking if you still had some time free before you had to be home. There's something I'd like to show you. Unless you're busy right now. I promise I won't take more than an hour of your time."

It wasn't a good idea, she mused. Being with him, one on one, allowing herself to get closer in any way when she knew the risks. But the heart of her problem with Blake had only increased over the last seven years.

Nothing in life was as good as being with him. At least this time, she had the excuse of wanting to work out Blake's best possible relationship in her son's life. It was a good excuse. A real one.

But her heart wasn't wildly thumping like an exuberant puppy's tail because of Nate when she said yes.

# Six

Serena could find her way around the Whitehorn countryside if she were blindfolded, so she recognized the general area where Blake was driving but not why he chose to stop his car at this specific hillside.

"You know where we are?" Blake asked her.

Serena hated to point out the obvious. "Well, sure. God's country."

He chuckled. "I'm well aware that you love Montana."

"Who on earth wouldn't?"

"In this case, I was just trying to ask if you were familiar with this piece of land and who it belonged to."

"Familiar, no." She shot him a wry grin. "I've trespassed every inch of private road I can think of over the years, on horseback or foot, but somehow I must have missed this beauty of a stretch. But since we passed a sign for the Kincaid ranch a while ago, I assume we're still on Kincaid property?"

"Yes and no. Yes, it was originally part of the Kincaid ranch. But the reason I brought you to this spot was because I thought it would be of specific interest to you. And Nate.'' On that enigmatic note, the blasted man turned the key to shut off the engine and apparently thought he could change the subject. ''Do you have time to walk? Won't take ten minutes to show you what I'd like you to see.''

''What do you mean, of interest to Nate?''

''I'll explain. But first let me show you.''

She climbed out of the car when he did, thinking that they both needed cowboy boots rather than summer sandals to walk this kind of rough terrain. But then Blake offered his hand for hers to take.

She did, feeling his fingers tent with hers, feeling the pulse in the heart of his palm. She'd have walked barefoot over coals for that feeling, and before they'd crested the first knoll, he suddenly clutched hard. She glanced at him, thinking maybe he was feeling the same heart pull she was—but no, he was just trying to communicate a be-silent message to her.

Their human scent had startled a mule buck deer. A mere fifty feet away, the beauty stood frozen, his sleek supple hide catching the pale sunlight, so young its antlers were still covered in velvet. As soon as the buck worked up his courage, he scampered off. Blake grinned at her. She grinned back and, swinging hands, they clambered up a rock-studded knoll.

This time in August, this part of Montana inevitably looked a little parched and crinkled around the edges, but not everywhere. From the top of the knoll she could see the granite gray of the Crazy Mountains in the west, the sages and khaki greens of the valley

stretching south and east. But scattered in the rolls
and tucks of the land were surprises—a fat, gnarled
cottonwood shading an emerald patch of grass. There
had to be water, even if she couldn't see it, because
beyond that bosomy roll was another verdant field
kicking up color everywhere—pink bitterroot, purple
pasqueflowers, and the shine of some yellow blossom,
all swaying like flirting girls in the evening breeze.
Above it all was a nonstop blue sky that was as big
as a soul—and always had owned a corner of hers.

"I hoped you'd like this. But the sun's glaring right
on the eyes, too hard to see. Let's climb down a bit."
Heat still sizzled in the air as he led her down to the
shady side of the hill. The road disappeared from
sight. Somewhere in the somnolent early evening was
the dripping scent of some sweet wildflower. Most of
the terrain was still drenched with sunlight, but now
she could see, in the cleavage of two shaggy hillsides,
the sparkle of silver water. The stream wound around
a stand of western larch that would turn solid gold in
a few more months.

"It's a gorgeous piece of land, Blake," she murmured, yet she couldn't help looking at him curiously.
She'd always been the nature lover, not him. His
whole world had always been inside, his drive to become a doctor overshadowing anything else in life.
She was the one who tended to half live outside, drink
the sunlight, breathe in the scent of grass, and feel a
spiritual pull stronger than in any church.

Yet just then, he seemed tuned to one of nature's

spiritual channels, too. Although his left hand was still grasping hers, his gaze swept from east to west, inhaling the landscape, savoring the countryside. And then his eyes suddenly dropped to hers. She saw the warmth in his gaze, felt it catch like kindling on a stark winter's night.

"Do you know the story of my father?" he asked her.

"I know the gossip that's been spread in town. But how much of that is true, I have no idea."

"Well, I hate to bore you with family history, but I don't know any other way to give you the whole picture. Back in the 1920s, the Kincaids came to Blue River County and picked this site for their ranch. The patriarch of the clan was Caleb Kincaid. He had two sons, Zeke and Bart, and they read like the Cain and Abel story, one good brother, one bad. Zeke was the bad one, screwed Bart out of his share of the ranch, after which Bart moved away and settled west of here. Bart had a son, Garrett. My blood grandfather."

"Most of that I'd heard," she admitted. "Kincaids have been too important to this area for folks not to talk about your kin."

"Well, your kin was here first—in the obvious sense that Native Americans roamed this area before any hooligan upstart whites settled here. And to me, that makes it even more right that Nate know something about this particular stretch of property."

"That's the second time you implied that Nate has

some connection to this land. But I still don't understand what you mean.''

Blake sighed, as if exasperated with himself for taking so long to express himself clearly. ''I'm sorry, but I'm stuck explaining more family history to get to the point. Once Zeke—the-bad-brother Kincaid—took over the ranch, the other side of the family lost touch, quit communicating for years. Then Garrett, my grandfather, read some newspaper article about Wayne Kincaid. That was the first Garrett knew any blood kin from Blue River County was still alive. The two men set up a meeting, got together—for which Garrett brought along his grown son, Larry.''

''Larry. Your dad,'' Serena echoed carefully, not sure how much he wanted to get into or talk about.

''Yeah. A lot of this history would never have happened if Larry Kincaid hadn't settled here, gotten married and raised so much hell. Garrett didn't know about his son's shenanigans until after Larry died. That was when Garrett found papers in Larry's safe-deposit box referring to a number of illegitimate children, including my brother and me. But in the meantime, over the years, Garrett and Wayne Kincaid became close, established a warm family relationship. So when Wayne realized that he needed to put the ranch up for sale, my grandfather was the first one he told. And Garrett leaped to buy it. Not because he wanted to ranch himself—and certainly not at his age—but because he saw acquiring the land as a chance to right some serious old wrongs.''

"I take it that Garrett has the same strong sense of justice as his grandson? It sounds like we're talking an inherited trait," Serena gently teased.

Blake motioned her to sit, as he eased down to the ground himself and stretched out his long legs. "Garrett may be a saint, but you know better than anyone that I'm not. I do admire my grandfather, though. Liked him from the first day we met."

"Yeah, me, too. And I don't know anyone in the community who doesn't think a lot of your gramps." Once she sat down, the sun was no longer in her eyes, and she studied Blake—the bandage on his left hand, the rip in his khakis. He hadn't complained about anything hurting after his crashing encounter with cement, but she knew his left palm had been badly skinned. The grass was calf-tall, ticklish on her bare legs, and when Blake leaned back, so did she. The earth smelled verdant and sun-warmed, the evening turning drowsy and still, the wildflowers started to blur in the predusk light.

"Well, the thing is, the reason Garrett wanted to buy the ranch was to be able to give it away. His plan was to give a slice to each of his illegitimate grandchildren. He brought all of us together at the ranch in May for a reunion. That was the first most of us knew that we were related. Garrett talked about wanting the land to be a touchstone for all the brothers. He already know most of us wouldn't want to ranch it. That wasn't the point. He wanted us to have a piece of the home base, a place of belonging, a concrete part of our Kincaid family heritage.''

"So this section of your land is your share?" Serena asked.

"Technically, yes, although it'll be a while before I have the deed. When I had dinner with Garrett a few nights ago, he mentioned that there's been a legal problem suddenly kicked in. You may have already heard the gossip about it in town. A guy named Jordan Baxter has a long grudge against the Kincaid family, and he's managed to hold up the sale by claiming rights to a small parcel that the Baxter family once owned. I don't know how that's going to turn out, but it doesn't affect this particular parcel of land anyway. Baxter isn't contending anything about this piece. It's just that all the paperwork's on hold until his claim goes through the court system.''

"Okay...." She'd listened intently, yet was still unsure why Blake felt it so important to tell her this whole story. As the sun drooped like a leaden ball, the air seemed to get smoky with dusk, heavier, softer. She loved seeing him against the backdrop of her sky, her country. He didn't look like a city doctor now. "So this is what you brought me here to see? Your land?"

He only made a minor correction in her comment. "What I brought you here to see was Nate's land."

"What?"

"I can't put Nate's name on the deed until the legal problem with Baxter and my grandfather is resolved.

But the minute that legal business is finished, this will all belong to Nate.''

Her breath caught. She couldn't remember feeling more overwhelmed. ''Blake, you don't need to do that! For heaven's sake, you just found out that you were a Kincaid instead of a Remmington, that this land is part of your own history. You'd be giving it up before you even had a chance to feel part of it.''

He shook his head. ''It never was and never will be mine in any way that matters, Serena. Garrett passed on the land to try and make up for what his son did—for being irresponsible, for carelessly bringing children in the world.'' His eyes met hers squarely. ''And now I find out that I've done the same thing.''

''You're nothing like your father!'' she said, fast, fiercely.

''As far as Nate, the similarity's inescapable. I contributed some sperm, but that's it. No different than my father hurt the women in his life. You got stuck with all the parenting, all the work, all the financial and emotional responsibility.''

''It's not the same! You didn't know!'' She could feel a stab in her heart like real pain. The more she was with him, the more she realized how badly she'd hurt Blake by not telling him about the pregnancy. She wanted to ask his forgiveness a million times over, but it wasn't that simple. She deeply regretted hurting him, yet she couldn't regret her silence. The two things weren't the same. Right or wrong, Serena knew in her heart that she'd made the best decision she was capable of making seven years ago. That she was wiser now wasn't worth a Las Vegas dollar and didn't help her know what to do for Blake or their son now. "There's nothing you should be feeling guilty about. Nothing, Blake."

"I do feel guilty. But that's not the whole story. When I started thinking about giving him this property, it just seemed right to me. For one thing, the land could be a trust for Nate. A legacy. Both roots and financial security, something of his own, something that belongs to him."

She looked at him softly. "But where does that leave you?"

"Me? I'm talking about taking care of Nate."

She nodded. "I understand. But our son is still a small child. And you barely had this land before you're trying to give it away. Don't you have the need yourself to belong to something or someone?"

For just an instant she saw the young boy's yearning in the grown man's eyes, as if for years Blake had hoped to belong to something, hoped to feel a part of something. But then he'd grown up and put aside his belief in Santa Claus. "I don't need the land or anything. There's also another reason—a more important reason—why I want Nate to have it."

"What?"

He gestured, as if wishing his hand could communicate what he didn't know how to say. "I want badly for Nate to know I'm his father, Serena. But this gives both you and Nate a choice. If you feel my being part of his life isn't a good thing for him, then he'll still have this land. Always. Forever. And that way he'd never have to accept me as his dad unless he actually wanted to.''

Serena didn't quite understand what he was getting at, only that it was obviously very important to him. ''Blake, you are his father. You don't have to prove anything.''

''I think I do.'' He ran a hand through his hair. ''Can you understand? Essentially I had two fathers, but the one never gave a damn if I existed and the other never acknowledged me. I know exactly how much fathers can hurt sons. And this is one way I can make absolutely positive that never happens to Nate. I can give him a choice about whether he wants me in his life, partly because, by owning this property, he'll always have security. He won't need anything materially. And neither will you.''

''That's wonderful, but no. It's not necessary. And it's just too generous.'' Serena kept thinking that security wasn't the issue that Blake was making it out to be. The real issue was those dark heart corners where Blake had always been unwillingly vulnerable. As a kid he'd tried forever to win Harold Remmington's love and couldn't...only to discover that his blood father had never sought contact with him, either.

Maybe those wounds were scarred over, but they weren't forgotten. Blake had never felt valued, not by the adult men in his life. And now he seemed to see the land as a way to guarantee that Nate could have proof of a father's love, or more to the point, that Nate would never have to seek a relationship with a father who wasn't worth it. These were such dark, troubling issues for Blake that Serena was startled to see a sudden smile from him.

Her refusing his offer seemed to strike Blake's sense of humor. She caught a hint of a crooked grin, a winsome lightening in those dark blue eyes. "Well, honey. I hate to tell you this, but I wasn't asking your permission. I'm afraid this is how it's going to be. The property's going in Nate's name, with you listed as guardian, as soon as the legal rigmarole is over with. But I did want to tell you now. Just in case something happened to me before the papers are signed. I want both you and Garrett Kincaid to know what I want." He suddenly glanced at his watch, realized that he couldn't read the dial in the dusky light, and promptly stood. "Hell, I should have realized how late it was getting. We've got to get you back for Nate."

She stood, too, but her eyes were on him. She couldn't be less worried about being on time. Her brothers would never leave Nate alone if for some reason she wasn't there.

"Blake?"

"Yeah?" He hooked his right hand securely with hers, as if assuming she suddenly realized that the uneven path tended to be unpredictable in the murky twilight. "I should have noticed how dark it was getting. But it's not that far to the car—"

"Wait."

Immediately he stopped with an amenable smile, clearly waiting for her to say whatever was wrong.

But it wasn't that simple. Nothing was wrong. It was just that her mind's eye kept replaying the picture of Blake, his eyes, his face, when he motioned to the sprawling land. He was a doctor, not a lumberjack. A healer, not a cowboy. He'd never been that all that interested in nature, but at that moment she'd seen how he loved it. It had been in his eyes, the joy of it, the joy of this land, of it belonging to him, of having a treasure of a haven such as this. And that feeling of haven was obviously something he'd never had in his life.

Only how fast, how blasted fast, he was giving it away. To do the right thing for Nate and for her. Serena couldn't let it go.

"If you want to give this to your son, you can. As long as it's in your name and Nate's. Not mine."

He shook his head, swiftly, surely. "That wouldn't solve the same thing, Serena. I want it to be security for you, too. And I want the property to give Nate a choice. Like I said, the kind of choices I never had. No, none of us can choose who we're related to. But this way he'd never need me for any material reason. He'd be secure on his own. He'd never have to have a relationship with me, unless I'd proven to him that I'd be the kind of father he wanted to be with."

"Damn it, Blake. You think I'd raise a fool for a son?"

His jaw dropped, his expression twisted in confusion. "Well, no, of course not. I never meant—"

Serena knew he'd never meant to criticize her. He was criticizing himself. Making it sound as if he were unworthy as a father—so unworthy that he had to prove himself to her and Nate, as if he were auditioning for a job. By his life rules, he was being completely logical.

By his sense. By his logic. But not by hers.

She pulled him closer. Loving him had never been sane or wise. But it had always been right, the way reaching for him right now was right.

Blake had hungered his whole life to belong, to feel worthy of love. On the surface—in school, in life— he wore confidence in face and style. Yet, on the inside it wasn't there; he never felt good enough. He was no longer a child, searching for acceptance. As a man he lived by his own code, coped in his own way. But, Serena thought, he still needed to be loved.

He still believed himself unlovable.

And if she wanted to kiss him silly, she was damn well going to.

Blake couldn't understand it. How on earth could he have unleashed such a catastrophe? He hadn't touched her, except for courtesy gestures, even though touching her had been on his mind. Even though the look of her mouth and memories of her warm, soft skin and the pleasure sounds she made had invaded his head in nonstop replays. He'd let her alone. The way he was supposed to. He'd done what was right. His relationship with her and Nate mattered way too much to risk doing anything wrong.

Yet one instant the sun had been sneaking down the hillside and the next she was suddenly in his arms. One instant she tilted her face up and the next his mouth was taking hers, tasting hers, slammed on hers like a snap for its catch. One instant his bandaged left hand was swinging in midair as he walked and the next it was hooked around her neck like a noose, pulling her closer, pulling her in, the crushing swell of her breasts igniting every hormone he'd ever had and some that he hadn't known existed.

Eyes, shocked and startled, met his for all of a long, liquid second. Then that was it. She closed her eyes and seeped right into that kiss again. Her lips were softer than butter. Her tongue whispered against his, teasing, taunting. He heard her sigh, the sound of a jeweled promise. *I remember you.*

And the answering sigh from deep inside his belly. *And I remember wanting you like my whole body was on fire. And then, oh man. I remember having you.*

It was just like before. On that long-ago night he'd been wallowing in despair so deep he couldn't seem to swim out of it, grief over losing his mom mixed with a loneliness, a feeling there was no one out there, just a dark abyss. And then Serena had stopped by. A half hour later…hell, he never knew what hit him.

*She* had. He could have sworn sex had never been on his mind, yet he'd been all over her faster than a match could strike flame. She couldn't heal him. No one could. The sadness was still his problem to deal with, waiting for him...but not then. For those few hours there'd been nothing in his head but fire and smoke, and everything that burned had her name on it.

Now it was the same fire. The same burn. The same who-cared-if-the-moon-exploded. If he could just have her...one more time. One more minute. One more anything, as long as it was Serena.

His left hand was a bandaged mitt, yet somehow her blouse buttons loosened. Somehow the snap on her white shorts unclipped. Somehow that long, neat braid of hers started coming apart. Like his mind, her hair started unraveling and loosening, and suddenly there was silk. Heavy, rich silk shimmering over his fingers, through his fingers, and when he clutched her hair, she angled her neck even more responsively, allowing him to kiss her deeper, more possessively.

He realized that it was too uncomfortable for her to stand, straining her neck that way. It was easier, much easier, when he lowered them both to the ground. The raw scrape on his left thigh stung sharply, trying to distract him from the leftover memory of his encounter with the asphalt street and cement curb earlier that day. But he'd never have met up with Serena if it hadn't been for that accident, so he was grateful for the scrapes and cuts. Grateful for the ticklish prairie grass, the rocky soil beneath, the sudden hushed coolness as the moon started rising and they dipped out of sight of man or mountain, cleaving together in the soft shadows. Her breast filled his hand, firm, full, the tip swollen and hot in the nest of his palm, her heart slamming against him. She wanted...

Him.

It amazed him seven years ago, and stunned him even more now. He was a good man and a good doctor; he knew that. But the people closest in his life never seemed to find much motivation to love him, to want him around. Except for her. She fired up for his kisses the way a furnace lived for a winter blizzard. Her long supple body swayed into his, melding close, melting close, as if she belonged to him.

Both were breathing as if desperately short of oxygen. She rubbed against him, inviting more intimacy. He was achingly hard and primed. Too primed. Until that moment he had no idea how long he'd been suffering from Serena deprivation. He hadn't been with her in seven years. That was a long time to be without sunlight, without sustenance, especially when he knew exactly how fiercely, how wildly, he wanted her. Flat, beneath him. Flowing into her, claiming her, drowning her in every tenderness he owned, every prowess he claimed, every skill he'd ever dreamed of.

"Blake?"

He heard the question in her voice. The demand. "Shh."

"Blake. Yes. Now. Yes."

"Too rough. The ground is too rocky—"

"I don't care."

"It's late."

"I don't care."

"I could hurt you."

"I don't care."

Hell, he didn't know where the sudden burst of sanity came from. He sure didn't appreciate it, but it was like a bee sting to his mind, the kind of mean, stinging hurt he just couldn't ignore.

Their making love just wouldn't be right. It mattered more than life to him to be good to her. To do the right thing this time—for her, for Nate. What the two of them—the three of them—could have together was too important to risk screwing up just because he had a small problem like dying from wanting her.

He severed the kiss, then tried to practice breathing the way a decent man breathed—in, out, taking air in instead of inhaling her as if she were more than his survival oxygen. He clenched his jaw, removed his hand from her breast, then covered her with the white linen shirt she was wearing. He tried to button it, but with his bandaged hand he couldn't. At least, he could still make sure sights weren't adding to his temptation. He pulled up her shorts, thinking this had to be penance, when two seconds before he could have had it all.

She was still saying yes with her eyes as she sat up and started buttoning her shirt. Her gaze still glazed his face. He saw warmth, need, fire in those sensual eyes. But he also saw wariness, as if Serena were waiting to be hurt.

"I want you," he whispered fiercely. "If it were up to me, I'd never stop in this lifetime."

"But you did stop. You're the one pulling back."

"Only because I'd have to shoot myself if I caused you regrets a second time, Serena."

"I didn't have regrets the first time."

"You had a son that neither of us planned. A pregnancy that upended your whole life. And I don't know where you and I are headed this time. I just know one thing. I won't risk hurting you again if I can help it."

When they climbed into his car a few minutes later and he leveled the accelerator, speeding for her place, Blake kept thinking gloomily that it was exactly the same as it had been before. Around her, he wanted to be good. The best man he was capable of being. Instead, he seemed doomed to be wicked, to do the wrong thing.

Worse yet, he mused, he loved that feeling of being wicked with her.

But that wasn't good enough. Blake had a taste of the future now—and a hope they actually might have a future together. He could risk everything, for her and Nate, if he made mistakes. He needed to behave like a Boy Scout from now on, and that was that.

# HOW TO GET YOUR
# 2 FREE BOOKS AND FREE GIF

1. Peel off the 2 FREE BOOKS seal from the front cover. Place it in the space provided at right. This automatically entitles you to receive two free books and an exciting mystery gift.

2. Send back this card and you'll get 2 "The Best of the Best™" novels. These bo have a combined cover price of $11.00 or more in the U.S. and $13.00 or mc in Canada, but they are yours to keep absolutely FREE!

3. There's <u>no</u> catch. You're under <u>no</u> obligation to buy anything. We charge nothing – ZERO – for your first shipment. And you don't have to make any minimum number of purchases – not even one!

4. We call this line "The Best of the Best" because each month you'll receive the best books by the world's hottest authors. These authors show up time and tir again on all the major bestseller lists and their books sell out as soon as they the stores. You'll like the convenience of getting them delivered to your home our discount prices…and you'll love your subscriber newsletter featuring aut news, horoscopes, recipes, book reviews and much more!

5. We hope that after receiving your free books you'll want to remain a subscrib But the choice is yours – to continue or cancel, anytime at all! So why not tak us up on our invitation, with no risk of any kind. You'll be glad you did!

6. And remember…we'll send you a mystery gift ABSOLUTELY FREE just for givi "The Best of the Best" a try!

## SPECIAL
## FREE GIFT!

We'll send you a fabulous mystery gift, absolutely FREE, simply for acceptin our no-risk offer!

Visit us at
www.mirabooks.com

# Books FREE!

DETACH AND MAIL CARD TODAY!

**HURRY!** **Return this card promptly to get 2 FREE Books and a FREE Gift!**

*The Best of the Best*™

**YES!** Please send me the 2 FREE "The Best of the Best" novels and FREE gift for which I qualify. I understand that I am under no obligation to purchase anything further, as explained on the opposite page.

Affix
peel-off
2 FREE BOOKS
sticker here.

P-BB1-00
**385 MDL CY2W**                                    **185 MDL CY2X**

| | | | | | | | | | | | | | | | | | | |
NAME                         (PLEASE PRINT CLEARLY)

| | | | | | | | | | | | | | | | | | | |
ADDRESS

| | | | | | | | | | | | | | | | | | | |
APT.#                    CITY

| | | | | | | | | | | | | | | | | | | |
STATE/PROV.                         ZIP/POSTAL CODE

# The Best of the Best™—Here's How it Works

# Seven

Serena managed to be "accidentally on purpose" in the backyard with Nate when she heard the car pull into the drive. "Well, I'll be darned. It sounds like we have company," she said brightly.

"Nffgh."

Well, her son's grunt lacked a certain enthusiasm—he was having way too much fun with his rabbits to care about visitors. But Serena was determined to make this particular visitor feel welcomed if there was any possible way.

When Blake stepped around the corner of the house, her pulse galloped like a frisky colt's. But then she remembered her son, and swiftly, heartily, slapped a hand over her heart. "Why, it's Dr. Blake! What a surprise!"

Blake grinned and rolled his eyes, as if teasing her for hamming this up too hard. His stopping by this Saturday morning, of course, was no surprise. They'd had it planned since last Tuesday. Serena had mentally started dating everything from the Tuesday Night They'd Almost Made Love—as if that were the title on the only chapter that mattered in her life.

"Hey, Serena. Hey, Nate. Man, those are really cool rabbits." Blake's gaze took a long telephoto shot over her eyes, her mouth, her barefoot figure in a navy top and shorts. Her stomach flip-flopped in response to the promise of trouble she saw in his eyes, but he quickly turned away and hunkered down next to her son.

Nate glanced at him sideways as he continued feeding his long-eared babies prize carrots from his mom's garden. "You like rabbits?"

"I love rabbits," Blake assured him. "In fact, I'd like to play with 'em sometime, if you wouldn't mind."

"Sure. You just gotta watch Whiskey. The cats don't pay any 'ttention. But Whiskey…sometimes I think he'd like to catch my rabbits."

"I'll bet he would." Naturally the animals swarmed Blake the minute they spotted him. Whiskey was already drooling on his shoulder and one of the kittens was trying to climb up his pant leg. Clearly, though, the enthusiastic welcome he'd been hoping for wasn't from the pets. "Nate, there was a reason I stopped by. I can see you're busy, but when you're done feeding your rabbits, I thought maybe you and your mom might like to go sailing with me for a couple hours this afternoon."

Nate held a carrot midair, green top swinging. "Sailing? Like in a boat?"

"Yup."

"Wow. You mean, like really sailing? Like in a real boat?"

"Yes. It's a little boat, but definitely a real one."

"Mom, did you hear? Did you? Did you?" Nate's face whipped back to Blake's. "My uncles take me fishing a lot. I love fishing. But we fish from the shore, you know? Nobody in my whole life ever took me sailing." Another whiplash back to Serena. "Can we go, Mom? Can we? Can we?"

Serena pretended to consider, because it was so much fun watching her son build up anticipation, and even more fun watching Blake light up at Nate's response. "Sounds like a super idea to me."

"It is. I can swim, did I tell you, Dr. Blake? I can put my head under water and everything."

"No, you didn't tell me, but I'm not surprised you're so good. Of course, if you're in a boat, you have to wear a life jacket. I do, too. Even if you can swim, it's a good safety rule."

"Oh, that's okay. I love life jackets. My whole life, I loved life jackets. Piece of cake, right, Mom? Uh, Mom?"

"What, darlin'?"

"Do I have a life jacket?"

Typical of a child, Nate was talking as if Blake couldn't hear him. "I happen to have one just the right size for an extra-strong six-year-old."

"That's me, extra strong. How did you know?"

"I looked at you and thought, Boy, Nate's really big and strong."

"Well, you were right, Dr. Blake. Nobody's strong as me. You can ask my mom. Mom?"

Like the straight man in a comedy, Serena dutifully came through with her line about her son's Godzilla-like strength, but on the inside she was holding her breath. This excursion had been planned, which was why swimming suits and towels were heaped on the kitchen counter, ready to go. She'd never asked Blake where he'd found a sailboat to rent or what lake they were going to. None of those details mattered.

All that mattered was that, for the first time, her son wanted to go somewhere to be with Blake. For sure the boat ride was bribery. But he still wanted to go. He wasn't just being polite. He was talking non-stop to Blake with only a token comment directed to her—in other words, just occasionally needing to connect with Mom-the-safety-net—but Serena could see she wasn't really necessary. As she scooped up the supplies from the kitchen and stepped back outside, a shadow suddenly crossed overhead.

Instinctively she glanced up, saw a young—and so rare—bald eagle, its white head and velvet-brown wings catching the sunlight. She wasn't superstitious. It always burned her to hear about Native American stereotypes such as being chronically late, or unable to hold a glass of wine, or being overly superstitious. But it seemed sometimes she was pure Cheyenne, because that precious eagle just had to be a good omen.

"Okay, let's get everybody strapped in." Blake

opened the back door of the Acura for Nate to pile in, when Serena interrupted.

"Nate, you can sit in the front seat if you want."

"By Dr. Blake? Okay!"

She stashed the towels and sack of supplies in the back seat, but didn't get in herself. As if on cue, both males seemed to realize that she was standing outside and not moving to join them.

"Mom, aren't you coming?"

If her son had sounded the least upset, Serena would probably have popped right into the car. But Nate only sounded curious when he asked the question. It was big, strong Blake who suddenly looked panic-stricken. "Serena, you have to come."

Well, that had been the plan and until seconds ago Serena had never considered staying home. She wanted to go, wanted to be with both of them. But, darn it, this was the first shot her guys had had to bond. "Well, you know I'd love to come," she said smoothly, "but school's starting in just a few days. If you two were going to be gone for a couple hours, that would give me time to head over to the school and get some work done on my room. I'll be back here and have dinner ready by the time you guys get home."

"Okay, Mom. But it's your loss," Nate told her sadly. "Let's go, Dr. Blake."

Blake momentarily looked as stunned as a statue.

Man. It was all she could do not to whisk around the car to pull him into a hug. But a display of affection for Blake wasn't quite right around Nate—at least not yet—and right then, would probably only unsettle Blake even more. "You're going to be fine," she told him. "Have a great time, you guys. Nate, you watch out for Dr. Blake now. Don't let him do anything wild. And don't you guys pick up any girls!"

Nate started giggling. "Aw, Mom." He turned to Blake, "She's teasing, Dr. Blake. You can do wild stuff if you want. You're a grown-up. And I'll be good because we're going sailing. You can't imagine how good I'm gonna be. You can't."

She waved them off, her mind meandering back over the last week. Three times, she mused. Since that unforgettable Tuesday night, Blake had popped over three more times to see Nate—and each time had been a complete disaster.

She'd racked her brain trying to understand why. Yes, she could see that he was trying too hard and just couldn't seem to relax around Nate, but she'd been so sure that a little time would help the problem.

Wrong. The first occasion she'd put aprons on both of them and let them loose in the kitchen making cookies. What could possibly go wrong? She'd made the dough herself. All the guys had to do was mix it. By nature cookie-making was a terrific guy activity, because it involved making dreadful messes on a par with playing with mud. Only her guys had started licking the spoon a little too early and a little too much, and both had ended up with stomachaches.

The time after that, she'd set them up in the backyard with some basic science experiments. Again, the kind of thing all males enjoyed—making wedges and pulleys and levers. Serena used the experiments herself in some of her science classes, so she was positive that a six-year-old could pull off the concepts in a sandbox and that success would make him feel really cool. And it had worked just like that. For Nate.

But apparently the experiments were a little too challenging for a thirty-two-year-old Rhodes scholar to master.

Lastly, there'd been the kite episode. The afternoon had been sweltering hot, but there'd still been a wind, and not just a little fretful breeze, but a gusty wind tearing off the Crazy Mountains. As it happened, Nate had a fancy kite shaped like a cougar that he'd been dying to fly, and the day was one of those perfect ones when even a novice kite flyer could get it up in the air.

They'd gotten it up beautifully. The two guys had been shrieking together as they'd run through the fields. Only it seemed the cougar hit a teensy whirlwind and it had started nosediving and then crashed. One dead cougar kite.

Nate had recovered from the tragedy, but Blake had been inconsolable. Worse yet, her brothers, who had stopped by after that, had known how to mend the kite and Blake hadn't. He'd seemed to get on just fine with her family. Both her brothers liked him. But the doc was only trying to prove himself to one human in the universe—Nate—and so far nothing was cooking well with him. At least in his daddy's judgment.

Maybe this time, Serena hoped as she meandered back into the house. She'd fibbed about working at the school. The new school year was about to start next week, but she'd had her classroom long ready, which left her with several hours free. She put on "The Nutcracker Suite" at boom-box volume, lolled in a tepid bath, then ambled out to the kitchen in fresh jeans and a shirt to make dinner. Four o'clock passed. Then four-thirty. Then five. Then five-thirty.

She'd roasted potatoes in a clay pot, fixed some Prairie-rubbed chicken, buried some zucchini under so much cheese that Nate'd never realize there was a vegetable, threw together some blueberry muffins, then abruptly realized she was making enough food for ten people. She quit working and paced.

She set the table and paced some more.

When Whiskey and the cats started pacing with her, she fed the menagerie, sat with the kittens and a book, then got up and paced again.

Finally, just before six, she heard a car door slam. Her son, damp around the edges, hurtled in the house with pink cheeks and a big smile.

"Mom! Guess what! We tipped over! I had the best time in my whole life! I got all wet and we almost died! It was so much fun I didn't want to come home! You gotta go with us next time!"

"Wow, that sounds like quite a story."

"It is, it is! I can't wait to tell you and I'm starving and I have to go to the bathroom, too!"

"Okay, short stuff, hit the bathroom first then wash your hands. You and Dr. Blake can tell me the whole story over dinner."

By the time Serena was dishing up homemade peach ice cream, she'd heard the story at least six times, each version more extensively embellished than the last. Nate was talking so nonstop that she'd had no chance to engage Blake in any conversation, much less realize that something was seriously wrong. When she handed him his bowl of ice cream with a dollop of marshmallow on top, he shook his head.

"Dinner was wonderful. Couldn't have been better, but I'm really full now."

He couldn't be full. Normally he had an army-size appetite, but his dinner plate was barely touched and now he was turning down the most famous home-made ice cream in the county. Serena kept trying to get a serious look at him, but there was just no tuning down her exuberant son.

"Mom! Did I tell you the part about when we tipped over?"

"Uh-huh, I do believe you did, but I have the feeling you want to tell me again."

He did. And Serena listened, yet again, to how Blake had trusted him for approximately a second and a half to hold the jib and then, like a ride at the carnival, the boat tipped and they ended up in the water with the boat on top of them.

"I cried for a second because I was a little scared. But just a little, and Dr. Blake said I was being brave even if I did cry. I wasn't going to tell you about that part, Mom. But it wasn't for long, anyway. We were in the middle of the lake in the middle of nowhere and I thought we were going to die!"

"Wow," murmured Serena, this time as she tucked him into bed a good two hours later. Nate was so whipped he could hardly keep his eyes open. The story was still getting replayed, still with exclamation marks, but yawns were making up more and more of the punctuation. Whiskey and the kittens had snuck up onto the bed and were still valiantly attempting to listen from various hiding points in the blanket folds. "Okay, lights out for everyone now. You can tell me about it again tomorrow, okay?"

"Okay. I love you, Mom."

"I love you, too. Sleep tight, lovebug."

Back in the living room, though, the silent Dr. Blake now seemed to be wearing a hole around her hearth. The easy, reassuring smiles for his son were gone. His hands were jammed into his shorts' pockets, his forehead dented with a serious frown, his skin pinched with stress.

"Serena, I didn't want to say anything in front of him, but..." He hesitated. "Let's go outside."

"Okay." Understanding that he didn't want Nate to overhear them, she grabbed the couch throw so they could sit on the lawn. It was a good night for it. A breeze was crisping out of the west, chasing away the bugs, cooling off the mean heat of the day. One kitten had followed them out and curled up on Serena's stomach when she laid back. Blake lay back on his elbows, about as relaxed as a rabbit in lion's paw range.

"You have to be upset with me," he started baldly.

"Upset?"

"Serena, I'd have shot myself before knowingly exposing Nate to any danger. We had life jackets on and there was barely a breeze, so it's not like we were flying across the water. Sailing was one of the few things I took up in California, and I swear I know what I'm doing."

She saw those blue eyes, so full of emotion, so full of storm. His muscles were all tensed and bunching in his forearms and shoulders. "Blake, hold on there. You think I'm angry with you about something?"

"Obviously. For putting Nate in jeopardy. But it didn't happen quite like he said."

"Of course it didn't."

"Of course?" For an instant he looked blank, as if trying to comprehend that she didn't buy a six-year-old's version of any story wholesale. Then he sucked in a breath. "Look, Serena, this is what really happened—"

"I don't want to know."

"Pardon?"

She knew she'd startled him again. But all this time, *this* was the Blake she'd fallen for. The Blake who felt life and emotions so deeply. Although he was a contained man, and never would be one to re- veal his feelings easily, she'd always respected that. But years ago she'd understood that the right woman could matter to him. Blake needed someone he could be himself with; that freedom to let go didn't seem to be something he could give himself. Seven years ago, the realization that she had the power to do something good for him had given her a feeling of rightness inside as nothing else ever had.

He began again. "I want to tell you—"

"No." She leaned over and lifted a hand to his cheek. That slight gesture was enough to make his eyes darken and his body still. "There's nothing I need to know, except what I already figured out. You two had a great time together today. You enjoyed him—"

"Well, yeah, of course I did, but—"

"—and he enjoyed being with you. I was begin- ning to worry you'd never loosen up and just be your- self with him, Doc."

He was trying to whisper, obviously for Nate's sake, but his hissed bass voice had the ragged hem of impatience. "That's what I'm trying to tell you! I loosened up. And we capsized a boat. This is not something you need to be understanding about, for God's sake."

"I'd trust Nate in your hands any day of the week. If any type of accident had to happen, I'd be relieved to find out he was with you, because I'd trust you to handle it better than anyone else."

"Serena, you're not listening to me! I'm trying to tell you that I screwed up."

"And I'm trying to tell you that you didn't. So forget it."

"Damn it…"

It wasn't she who initiated a kiss this time. And for darn sure, she wasn't expecting it. Blake just suddenly pounced, as if too exasperated to think of any other way to make her quit arguing with him. The kitten snoozing between them screeched when she suddenly found herself squished. Serena felt like screeching, too.

There he was. The Blake she remembered. Naked, not physically, but heart-exposed, the kind of naked that mattered. Yeah, she felt the crush of frustration when his mouth first met hers, but that anger was gone faster than a puff of wind. He lifted his head. She heard a man's sigh, half groan, half wooing call, guttural and low. And then he gathered her up, claiming her mouth again, his hands taking in the scent and shape and texture of her, his leg reaching over to wrap hers under him.

Suddenly they were body to body, lover-close, only a few scraps of cotton between them. She could feel the heat of the sunburn on his chest from that afternoon, still smell the lakewater freshness, taste the tang of her minty iced tea he'd gulped at dinner. It struck her as funny that her son had told an incessant tale about a boat capsizing when that was precisely what was happening to her.

She was capsizing. Over Blake. Dipping over, tipping over, falling deep underwater, with nothing to hold on to but him.

There was nothing she wanted to hold on to but him.

He sighed again, this one darker, growlier. A hand swept up her side, skidding over her ribs, smoothing over her breasts, then pausing. His heart hiccuped against her and then his head dipped down. A tongue shivered across her throat, damp-kissing the vee of her shirt, parting the cotton. A button obligingly opened and his lips directly connected with her breast. Connected, and then settled in, slow and lazy, as if just maybe he never intended lifting his head ever again.

Instinctively she pulled the light blanket over both their heads. There were no neighbors in sight, no cars going by this late on a somnolent evening, but that wasn't the point. The point was the intimacy pouring off of Blake, the intensely private way he was kissing her. Those kisses were all hers. Only for her. Vulnerability was never anything he willingly exposed.

Under the blanket, because it was darker, he seemed freer. So did she. Limbs tangled with limbs; her kisses tangled with his kisses. Grass tickled where it touched bare flesh, and more bare flesh was exposed. Earth scents permeated the darkness, and more than anything she felt his smooth hands, taking, giving, learning her, inspiring her. Desire fired like an engine, heating up, revving up, smoking as it urgently charged up speed.

"Serena." He just said her name. But she heard longing, need, belonging. A question.

"Yes." She whispered it, groaned it. The word said everything.

Yet he suddenly closed his eyes for one agony of a second and then abruptly pulled away—not far, still next to her, but his hands moved away from dangerous territory. She could hear his breathing in the quiet night, hear her own. He yanked off the blanket, allowing them both cooler air. The watery twilight sky wasn't bright enough to make her blink, but it was still a smack of reality after the private darkness. Their private darkness.

Serena squeezed her eyes closed, the way he had, craving a moment's space, a moment to figure out what they were doing, what was going wrong, why he'd started this at all if he meant to pull away yet again.

His voice broke the silence. "I want you."

She turned her head. "And I want you."

"It's been building. I think about you all the time. Crave you. I imagine you when I go to sleep, then when I wake up. Serena, I'm not positive I can control it."

"And would that be so bad?"

Finally he turned his head. She saw the brilliance in his eyes, the tenderness when his gaze brushed her face. "I screwed your life up once. I'm not doing it again."

"What? You're the only one with a vote?"

He flashed a brief grin at her teasing, but it didn't last. "We both have a vote. I'm not saying that I know what's best for you. I'm just saying that I was guilty of being careless of you once. For the sake of my own conscience, I can't live with being careless of you again. If we're going to make love, I want us to talk about it. Ahead. Before I've got my hands on you."

"All right. And I agree. So you talk first, Doc."

But he was quiet for some long, heart-ticking moments. No sounds intruded on the night but the muted symphony of crickets and cicadas. "An affair around Nate would never work. He's too old, too aware. I'd like to think we're headed for a future. Not an affair, but the whole kahuna, rings and honeymoons and everything that goes with it." Again, his gaze touched her face, as sensually as a physical caress. "I'm not asking a question right now, Serena. Right now I don't know how either of us could be sure where we're headed. But that's just it. I'm wary of complicating your life too far, without feeling more sure that I've proven myself to Nate."

Serena swallowed. She wanted to leap up and soar, understanding full well that Blake was thinking of marriage. And so was she. But whether Blake was motivated by love, or still driven by responsibility, she still felt completely unsure. "Blake, you brought this up before. But you are his father. You have nothing to prove. And you've spent plenty of time with him now. If you want to tell him who you are, I think we could do it—''

''No. Not yet.''

''Why?''

''Because—'' He washed a rough hand over his face. ''Because I don't feel I've earned a place in his life yet. And after today I assumed you'd feel the same way. Instead of making inroads with our son, I seem to be screwing up worse all the time.''

''Blake?''

''What?''

She asked carefully, ''Are you making excuses not to be involved with me?''

''What? Of course not.''

''Because it isn't a package deal. Our being lovers and your being a dad. The fact is that you are Nate's father. You can be in his life, whether you're in mine in an intimate way or not. But I'll tell you something, Blake.'' She pushed up to her knees. ''I don't want guilt in my bed. I'm not asking for a ring. I'm not asking for anything. I believe as you do, that if two people are going to be involved, they either need to be married or very careful that a child doesn't know. But as far as my feelings about love, I don't think it works for anyone unless both give it a two-hundred-percent shot. So don't kiss me again if you're going to wring your hands about it not being right.''

''Serena, I've hurt you somehow. I can see it in

your face. I wasn't 'wringing my hands,' as you put it—"

She stood, putting distance between them so that she didn't hurt quite so much. "You've lost the joy, Blake."

"The joy? I don't understand."

"It's in you. A huge emotion. A huge capacity for love. I felt it seven years ago. I feel it when you touch me now. But if you don't want to feel that joy with me, then don't mess with my heart."

She walked swiftly, quietly, toward the house. He'd follow her, she knew, but for just that second, she could feel tears aching in her eyes. She'd hoped so hard for this second chance with him. And was still hoping.

But there was no way she could be with him if all he felt was responsibility. She'd grown up feeling beholden, loving but always owing her foster parents. Now she wanted love—or nothing. But if Blake didn't understand what she was asking him, Serena feared she was gambling her heart for stakes that could already be lost.

# Eight

Blake slouched low in his office chair, his bare feet on the desk. Nothing was quieter than a pediatrician's office at four in the morning, which made it an ideal place to hide from the world.

Outside, the night was still darker than a tomb. No birds were stirring, no mice, no nothing moving anywhere. Except for Blake, tapping a tongue depressor, end to end, on his desk.

He loved her.

Maybe that wouldn't be such a petrifying revelation, except that the image kept replaying in his head. Of the two of them rolling around on a blanket in her front yard, almost naked, almost making love. In front of the whole world, for Pete's sake.

The tongue depressor snapped in his hand. He just reached for another, and started drumming that one in a worried, fretful rhythm on the desk. The strange thing wasn't that he loved or wanted Serena. Hell, any man would fall for a woman as beautiful on the inside and the outside as she was.

The strange thing was that she wanted to make love with him. Odder yet, considering that she'd heard the whole story about the sailing incident. Blake couldn't think of one thing he'd done right for Nate from the boy's conception. Yet instead of shooting him for nearly drowning their son, she'd essentially praised him for messing up with Nate yet again. Furthermore, they'd come two seconds away from making love. Where the hell was the woman's head?

The tongue depressor snapped in his hand. He dropped it onto the growing pile in his wastebasket, then slouched deeper in his chair. He kept trying to think, only his brain kept floating off to never-never land. Damn. Realizing he loved her was such a soul-blistering shock. And the enormity of the emotion swelling through him...well, it was obvious to Blake that no one else in the universe had ever experienced it before or could possibly understand. Sure, couples fell in love all the time. Undoubtedly they believed their kind of love was really something, but they didn't know. No man could possibly feel as strongly for a woman as he did for her.

Technically, Blake kept telling himself that it was a good thing. That he was out of his mind in love. That he was so crazy about her he couldn't think, much less sleep or eat. Except that the way Blake had always seen life, a man did the right thing—and the way a guy handled fatherhood was a critical judgment of whether he passed the Good Man test. A child was better off orphaned than stuck with a dad who didn't love him and constantly made him feel inadequate and unwantable. Then there was that other kind of lethally hurtful father. The kind who screwed around with women and never looked back to see if there were consequences. The kind of father who could make a child believe that he was as important as trash in a wastebasket.

As it happened, Blake had had both kinds of fathers.

And there was the bullet wound of the problem. He couldn't seem to stay away from Serena any more than he could stop breathing. But unless he could be a decent father, a provably decent father, he had no business knotting himself any tighter in Serena's or Nate's lives.

An odd, muffled sound at the private back door made Blake raise his head impatiently. He had to be imagining the knock. No one could possibly be here at this hour.

Another heavy-knuckled rap had Blake frowning and heaving out of his chair, putting on his shoes. When he unlatched the back door, the single security light in the parking lot illuminated the tall figure of a man, half hidden in the shadow of a tree. He stepped forward.

"Dr. Remmington? I saw your light under the blinds. Thank God, I found you alone. I need your help."

"I..." Blake searched his mind, trying to apply a name to the face. The night was eerie with black shadows and endless crickets and the moon glowing on dew-shiny grass. The man was a Native American.

At least six feet and about thirty years old. His black hair was short, worn almost in a Wall Street cut, conservative for these parts, though the dark shirt and jeans made him fit right in. In his arms, he carried a bundle incongruously wrapped in a pink and aqua blanket. ''I'm almost positive that I've met you, but I'm sorry, I don't remember...''

Blake waited for the man to fill in his name, yet a yawning silence hung between them for several moments. The stranger met his eyes, as if encouraging Blake to look and study all he wanted. From the clothes to the posture to the intelligence in the man's face, this just wasn't a man that Blake would expect to find skulking in shadows. And yes, he saw the tension and anxiety in those quiet, dark eyes, but it still took time before the other man willingly spoke.

''My name is Gavin Nighthawk. Dr. Nighthawk. I'm a surgical resident...and no, you haven't met me, but you probably recognize me from doing rounds at the hospital. That's how I knew you, and why I'm coming to you. I need another doctor, but specifically I need someone whom I can personally trust.''

Blake didn't like mysteries, and something definitely wasn't making sense here. He didn't budge from the doorway. ''What's the problem?''

Nighthawk didn't try moving past him. ''The problem is that I need your help but I don't want anyone to know that I was here. I'd be willing to pay anything for your silence—''

''Don't be ridiculous. Money isn't an issue. The

reason for all this secrecy is. If you're asking me to do something illegal, you've got the wrong ma—'' Blake's gaze shot up at a sound that seemed to emanate from the bundle in Nighthawk's arms. "That's a baby?"

"Yes," Gavin affirmed.

"Hell. Come on, come on, bring him in here right now." Knowing there was a child involved instantly shifted Blake's priorities. He hustled the other man inside, closed the door, and attempted to take the infant from Nighthawk's arms. Nighthawk resisted for several seconds, clearly reluctant to give up the baby. Again, he met Blake's eyes.

"That's what I heard. That I could trust you."

"You can trust me to obey the law. But I'm not going to fight about that with you now. Let's see the child." Blake was already unpeeling blankets as he strode into the nearest examining room and snapped on the light. "My God. This baby isn't more than hours old."

"I know."

"Whose is it?" Blake's entire attention now focused on his tiny patient, although he listened to Nighthawk's comments, which included both the questions the other man answered and those he failed to. Although Nighthawk may not realize it, information wasn't the only thing Blake was trying to figure out. For the sake of the baby, Blake wanted to understand everything about the baby's caretaker that he could.

"You'd think the last thing I'd need is another doctor when I obviously have medical training myself—but I haven't been around a baby this small since I was an intern. And the thing is, it wasn't a normal birth. The mother suddenly went into labor. This was in the middle of the woods. At night. She was upset, not expecting labor to start this soon, and...oh, God—"

Nighthawk's voice cracked like the sudden splinter of crystal. Blake kept quiet, tending to the baby, careful not to look at the other man. Nighthawk may not want to talk, but as far as Blake could tell, he badly needed to. He didn't look shaken, but he obviously was.

Bits and pieces of the story kept coming—not enough to give Blake a complete picture, but damn sure enough to make his heart clutch.

The young mother had asked to meet Nighthawk at a secluded spot in the wild virgin woods to the far west of the reservation. Obviously, Blake concluded, the two must have known each other, or why would the girl have asked to meet him? And why would Nighthawk have agreed to such a meeting?

Whatever had propelled the girl to contact Nighthawk, he'd gone to the woods having no idea that she was pregnant, much less that she was near term. According to Nighthawk, the young woman had been agitated and upset. So much so that he hadn't at first realized that it wasn't just emotional pain causing her tears and jerky motions but physical pain. The baby was coming. Fast. The young woman was terrified.

So was Nighthawk.

I would be, Blake thought, in the same circumstances.

According to Nighthawk, there'd been no time or way to get her out of the woods fast enough. The doctor couldn't see, wasn't sterile. Having no blankets, no drapes, and nothing but a knife on his key chain, he'd used his jacket for a mattress. Nighthawk's face was sweating, just trying to survive the telling of it.

"To be honest, the birth seemed to go fine. As good as it could possibly go—and for darn sure, fast. But everything started to worry me. I needed her checked out by another doctor, someone who knew babies and someone who wasn't as emotionally involved as I am. The circumstances of the birth just carried too many risks. I didn't have drops for the baby's eyes, no sterile clothes, nothing... Look, I just want you to examine her, all right? I—"

Blake was, and had been, examining the little one. "Where's the mother?" For the first time in quite a while, the examining room was completely silent. Blake looked up and pierced Nighthawk with a single stare. "I asked you, where is the mother?"

"Right now the issue is just the health of the baby."

"Is the mother sick? Was there excessive bleeding

after the delivery? Fever? Why didn't you bring her when you brought the baby?''

''I couldn't.''

For a moment Blake let that go. It was obvious from the razor-edged anxiety in Nighthawk's tone that the man had been pushed as far as he was willing to go, at least for the moment. And Blake didn't need two patients on his hands, until he'd figured out exactly what was going on with the first one.

''Well, you can stop worrying about the baby. Maybe she had a rough start in the woods, but she doesn't seem any worse for wear. You know what? Babies survived for centuries without us docs. Personally I think we're way overrated in the birth process.'' Instinctively Blake's voice had dropped to a calming, reassuring tone. For damn sure, he wanted more answers. But everything Nighthawk had said had also alerted Blake to the frantic worry in his tone. With Nighthawk being a surgeon, such panic could only have one reason. ''I take it you're the father.''

He heard Nighthawk suck in a breath, but not answer. Just as well. Temporarily, Blake had his hands full with the black-haired, dimple-cheeked, wrinkled-faced beauty. ''I see all ten fingers, all ten toes. Did your daddy tell you that you were gorgeous? I'll bet he did. Let's just see what you weigh, okay, sweetheart? Shh, I'll have you off there in a second.... Under five pounds. But just, and her lungs are strong, heart good. Babies have a faster heartbeat, which you know—or I'm sure you'd have remembered if you hadn't been shook up at suddenly discovering your-self to be a new father. I want the rest of the story on the mother.''

"It's better if you don't know."

"I want the story," Blake repeated. "Come on. You're a doctor yourself, so you know the law. If you attended a live birth, or even a stillbirth, you're re-quired to report it to the health department. If you fail to do that, you could face charges, even risk losing your license. And now you've made me part of this mess. For the record, I don't break laws. More im-portant than that, you know darn well that you de-scribed a potentially dangerous situation for the child. There's no possible way that I'm letting you take this baby unless I'm satisfied that she's going to be prop-erly taken care of. So start talking.''

Blake was increasingly worried about the whole story but not so concerned that he didn't swiftly, will-ingly, cradle the baby back into her daddy's arms. Something was obviously wrong, drastically wrong. But Blake had already made certain assessments, and how Nighthawk looked at the baby reinforced his characterization perfectly. The man was in love with his newborn. The protective and loving way he held the baby only affirmed for Blake that the bonding between father and daughter was as real as sunlight.

While Nighthawk held the baby, Blake had other things that needed doing. Without knowing where the nurses stocked supplies, he had to putter around the cupboards and cabinets. One cabinet stocked baby diapers of all sizes for the obvious reason—his teensy-size patients had the tendency to spring a leak while being examined. Sometimes moms were prepared; sometimes they weren't. Another cupboard stocked a variety of bottles and formula. The little one was starting to fret so Blake kept looking for a ready-to-feed bottle of formula. It took some time to find, which was just as well, since it took quite a while before Nighthawk finally found the courage to talk.

Blake almost had a heart attack—not when Gavin Nighthawk confessed to being the father which was as obvious as the sun rising in the morning—but when he admitted that the mother of the child was Christina Montgomery.

"You mean, the girl that's been missing? The girl the whole town's been talking about all week?"

"Yes."

The more Blake heard of the story, the less he liked it. Nighthawk claimed they'd never been a couple, just that this Christina had chased him hard for a while. One night when he was getting over a love affair gone sour, she'd come on to him and the obvious had happened. He'd had no idea she was pregnant, though, as she'd literally dropped out of his life after that. She had only contacted him a matter of hours ago, when she'd gone into labor and needed help. Apparently she'd kept the pregnancy a secret from everyone, including her family.

The whole story—true or not—bit on Blake's own conscience. It just hit too close to home. He'd turned to Serena once upon a time when his mind had been on his own problems. And he'd left her pregnant, no different than Nighthawk had left that young woman.

"So where is this Christina now?"

"She disappeared."

"Quit screwing around, Nighthawk. I need to know the answer. Why didn't you bring her in with the baby?" Blake looked at him. He wasn't buying his story.

Nighthawk gestured. "Christina had just given birth. She wasn't strong enough to walk out of the woods on her own. I needed to get both of them out of the elements and to a safe place, but I had no possible way to carry both at the same time. Both of us concluded the same thing, that as long as Christina wasn't in any immediate medical crisis, I should get the baby to safety first. So I took the baby, got her to a safe place, to someone I trusted. But it's not like I could do that in ten minutes. I couldn't get back to Christina for almost two hours—" His voice cracked.

"Take it easy." Blake could see Nighthawk's eyes hollow with stress. "Just tell me. What happened when you went back to her?"

"She was gone." Nighthawk swallowed hard. "There was no note. No sign of her. Nothing. I don't know if you're familiar with that area outside the reservation, but it isn't just woods and hills. There used to be sapphire mines around there. So many things could have happened. There was no excess blood on the scene, so I wasn't worried about her hemorrhaging from the birth, but where she could have gone, or why she would have left, I don't have a clue. She came to me for help, and God, I'd have given her help. But she went into labor so fast, I never got it all straight— what she was afraid of, why she was so upset and desperate.''

"Take it easy," Blake said again, even more gently.

"I can't take it easy. You wanted the story, but the whole story is I didn't know what to do. All I could think of was handling one crisis at a time, in order of priority. And my priority was the baby. I brought her to you because that was the most immediate critical thing—making sure she was all right.''

"She's beautiful.''

Nighthawk wasn't going to relax or let down his guard, but Blake saw the softening in those dark eyes for his daughter. "Yeah. She is, isn't she? Of course I examined her and she seemed okay, but...hell, I can't explain this. You'd think a doctor would have more confidence. But the more she seemed okay, the more I started worrying how ignorant I was about babies. And I just had no way to judge how difficult a birth in the open might have affected her. I had to be sure. She's my daughter.''

Damn but Blake was starting to like the man. Nighthawk said "my daughter" as if that explained the moon and the stars. Blake had felt the same way the instant he realized that Nate was his own.

"And there was another issue. Another immediate

priority, as far as I was concerned. If something happens," Nighthawk said, "I need you to be her doctor."

Blake warily stiffened again. "What do you mean, if something happens?"

"Remmington, come on. Like I've been trying to tell you—something's happened to Christina, but I don't know what, and I don't know why. I also don't know why she was so panicked that her family would find out about the baby. But the point is, right now this baby is her business and mine and no one else's. I'm not asking you to be quiet forever. Only long enough to give me some time. I need to find Christina and find out what's wrong on my own."

"Look. You're asking me to break the law. And surely you know that Christina's been listed as missing and everyone's been looking for her all week—"

"I'm only asking you to keep quiet for a short period of time. This baby isn't the law's business. Or Christina's father's business. Or anyone's business but hers and mine." Nighthawk's jaw clenched and unclenched, and then he sighed, heavier than a north wind and just as wearily. "I'll be honest—I don't know what the right thing to do is. I just don't want to cause Christina any more trouble than I already have. I promise you—I swear—I'll make sure the baby is loved and cared for. I just want the news about her and Christina kept quiet temporarily until I have a chance to straighten this out."

Blake hesitated. "What if you can't straighten it out? What if you don't find this Christina?"

Gavin met his eyes squarely. "I don't know. But can't you try to imagine yourself in my shoes? I've only been a father for a few hours. The mother of the baby is in some kind of trouble I don't understand, and just as bad, the baby could be in some kind of jeopardy that I don't know about. Do you hear me? I don't care about the law. I just care about making sure the baby's all right. And that Christina is, if I can find her."

"You're a stranger to me. I'm not risking my license, or breaking the law, without knowing you from Adam. I don't have a single reason to believe you."

"I'm still asking you to. Please, don't tell anyone that we were here."

"No."

"I don't want anyone knowing this baby exists yet."

"No."

"And I need you to be the baby's doctor if she gets sick or something happens. Until all this is resolved—"

"No!"

Damn. Nighthawk and the baby left minutes later, having gotten exactly what they wanted to out of Blake. A yes.

Doors started slamming around seven-thirty. By then the sun had long peeked over the horizon and was now beaming through the windows with beatific cheer. Blake had cleaned up, shaved, splashed ice water on his face, and was downing his second pot of coffee.

By the time the nurse cocked her head around the doorway to give him the morning's schedule, he bantered with her no differently than any other morning. No one guessed he was troubled. No one even guessed he was tired. Blake had never shown his problems and wasn't about to start now.

But on the inside, he felt as if his entire ethical system was falling apart in front of his eyes. His character, his morals, his integrity were all going to hell in a handbasket. Previously, his entire experience with lawbreaking consisted of a ten-year-old speeding ticket. He never bent the rules. He didn't know this damn Nighthawk from Adam, didn't have a shred of evidence the guy was telling the truth, didn't have a reason in hell to believe the father's plight...but he did.

It was Serena, Blake thought morosely. Nothing had been the same since he'd met up with her again. He'd become a stranger to himself. The one thing in his life he'd never doubted was his judgment, but lately he couldn't seem to tell right from wrong. All the blacks and whites were becoming blurry grays.

Patients came and went. More mothers cried than babies—which actually made it a pretty average day. His brother called, then his grandfather. Two four-year-olds broke out in a fistfight in the waiting room.

Blake suspected abuse with one of his little girl patients, but he couldn't prove it, and worrying about the child gave him a hammering headache by three.

Through the whole day, he kept trying to decide what the best thing would be for Serena. She needed something from him. Joy, she'd said.

Blake didn't have a clue what she meant, but it kept gnawing on his mind that she'd always seen him as a better man than he was. Two dads and one wife had found him easily expendable. It was only with Serena that he'd ever felt loved—but was she swayed by their mutual tie to Nate and five tons of chemistry?

Possibly the visit from Nighthawk was an omen, Blake considered. It seemed an ideal thing to confess to Serena. A way to show her what kind of man he really was. Fallible. Confused. Bumbling his way through the rights and wrongs of life...and just maybe, not the father she wanted for her son. But it seemed the only choice he had left was to be completely honest with her.

Serena rarely lost it. Heaven knew she'd long realized that she was highly emotional by nature, but losing her parents so young had indelibly changed her outlook on life. No matter how tough life was, she always remembered the agony of loss and loneliness from when she was little, and something inside her always reached for the joy instead of dwelling on the heartbreak.

Tonight, however, was the night before Nate's first

day of school and Serena's first teaching day of the new school year. In addition, she hadn't heard from Blake since arguing with him. She kept thinking he'd call, but not one of the five million calls she got was from the one person she wanted to talk to. She'd managed to get Nate ready for bed after dinner and had laid out his clothes for the sacred first day. But the time had kept running away, and she hadn't done anything to prepare herself for tomorrow. Adding to her fretful mood, rain was streaming from the sky like silver ribbons. Hot rain. No meanness to it, no lightning or wind. It bounced off the ground and snaked into rivers and just wouldn't quit. And at precisely 8:02 p.m., when she turned around to see the back door opening, her shriek could easily have been heard on the far side of the Tetons.

"What have you two done?"

Nate and Whiskey both stopped dead in their tracks. Boy and dog shared the same guilty expression. "Um, Mom…"

"Don't you 'um, Mom' me! Either of you!" Her finger wagged at the two of them—one wearing star-and-moon pajamas, but both equally drenched in mud. To add insult to injury, she heard the rap on the front door, not that she had time to answer it. "When did you two sneak back outside? You were clean. It's bedtime, for Pete's sake!"

"Mom, we just went out for a minute because Whiskey was hot. And the rain was so much fun and it felt so good. Only then we kind of slipped in this puddle. It was just an accident—''

''There was no accident. You rolled in the dirt! All I asked was that you stay clean. Now look at you! You're not just sopping wet but dripping mud all over the place. You're both going to have to get another bath—''

''Serena? Nate?''

Truthfully she'd heard the door open and sensed Blake walking up behind her, the same way she could sense her own heartbeat. But she was too busy losing it to have a coherent conversation. ''You're going to have to wait a minute,'' she said to Blake. ''I can't talk to you. I'm too busy murdering my son and his dog.''

''Is there any chance I could help before it comes to that?''

''Yeah, Dr. Blake, you could help!'' Nate piped up hopefully.

''Yeah, you can help,'' Serena said darkly. ''You can spank the pair of them after I finish murdering them both. And I mean to tell you, I am mad, Nate. You know you were all clean and supposed to be settling down before bed. You know I wouldn't have wanted you to go outside in the rain. Here it is eight o'clock and I have to clean you and Whiskey and the house all over again. And as far as rolling in the mud, young man—''

''I can give myself a bath, Mom.''

"No, you can't. Not when your hair needs washing and there's all that mud all over your ears."

"Then Dr. Blake wants to give me a bath, don't you, Dr. Blake? And I'll just tiptoe so I don't make any more messes. See, I'm only dripping a little now, Mom."

"Don't move. And, oh, my God, I forgot to hang up the phone. Are you still there, Victoria?" As soon as she hung up, the phone somehow managed to ring again. Perhaps Blake perceived that there was a slim chance she was inclined to hurl the receiver against the nearest wall, because he scooped it up before she could grab it.

"Would you mind calling back at another time? She really has her hands full here." That handled, Blake descended on the two culprits. "Whiskey, you're going out to the garage to dry off. We'll see about getting you clean a little later. And in the meantime, Nate, up."

Despite the mud, Nate scrambled up into Blake's arms faster than a monkey climbing a banana tree, looking so adorable that Serena almost—almost—forgot how furious she was. Dad and son looked like such a matched pair. A matched guilty pair, as they backed carefully, quietly, out of the room.

"I'm not through yelling at you! I'm not even close. I haven't even heard one apology and for that matter—"

"I'm sorry, Mom, really, really sorry!" Nate called.

Blake backed him up. "Look, Serena, we're both so sorry we can hardly stand it. But Nate and I are going to get out of your sight and get clean. You just sit down with a nice glass of wine, okay? Relax. Put your feet up. And I'll take care of the dog once I'm through with Nate."

Initially, there was too much to do to sit. But once she'd hosed down Whiskey and banished the dog to the garage to dry off, life started to look more recoverable. A mop took care of the dirt in the kitchen. By the time she'd made a mug of chamomile tea, she could hear the sounds of Blake and Nate giggling from behind the bathroom door.

Nothing could have relaxed her more than hearing those two having a great time together. She was stretched out on the living room couch by the time Blake finally emerged from the back rooms. By then, he'd put a spiffed-up Nate to bed and claimed the little one's eyes were already closed. She thought that she should probably explain her loss of temper. "Normally, a little mud doesn't bother me, but I think it was building up all evening, realizing that tomorrow is his first day of school."

"School?"

"Yeah. You know. My baby. His first day of school. He'll never be my baby the same way ever again."

"Um, Serena? I saw him covered with mud barely an hour ago. I don't think you need to worry that he's a full-fledged adult who doesn't need you as a mom anymore. Not today and not for quite a few years yet.''

He looked adorable, she realized. A few bubbles seemed to be clinging in a small blotch near his neck. He'd lost his shoes and was barefoot. His shirt was stained with mud, and several water spots were drying on his chinos. When he first came out and leaned over the couch, to find her prostrate and sprawled like a woman in a coma, he'd had the rare perception to not crack a smile.

''School's a terrible thing,'' she said sadly.

''You're a teacher. I thought you loved school.''

''I do, for heaven's sake. And God knows I'm trying to raise Nate so he'll be independent. Only I didn't mean for him to really grow up so much he'd be going to first grade.''

''Ah,'' Blake said, as if she were actually making sense. His gaze hovered on her mouth, then swiftly dropped to her mug. ''You need some more of that, whatever it is?''

''No. If I have any more tea, I'll probably float.'' Fascinating. His gaze had sneaked back up to her mouth again. ''I'm sorry. You got thrown into the middle of a war the minute you walked in.''

''I've never seen you lose your temper before. Remind me never to make you angry, okay?''

''Scared you, did I?''

''Oh, yeah. My knees are still shaking.'' But he hadn't stopped looking at her mouth yet. Or her throat. She no longer felt like lying on a couch with so much of her body exposed to his eyes, but he didn't move and she didn't want to call attention to herself by moving, either.

"Blake?"

"Huh?" His hand had lifted. His fingers seemed to be halfway to her cheek, about to touch her.

"You must have come over for some reason? Or was it just to stop by?"

The guilty hand dropped instantly, and though his eyes met hers, those wild, warm fires were abruptly banked. "You're right, I had a reason. There was something I needed to tell you."

"What?" She promptly sat up, for the first time noticing the odd, tenacious look in his eyes, as if he were stuck telling her bad news. "What's wrong?"

"Nothing, exactly." He hunched down on the far end of the couch. A deliberate distance from her, Serena thought. "I did something. Something I feel you should know about."

"Okay." Darkness was falling fast, the room turning a dusky velvet. The only light came from the lemony glow of a lamp in the far corner, and right when she wanted to see his expression clearly. She wasn't worried about whatever was troubling him. She was grateful. Blake had never brought her a problem before. As of that night on the lawn when they'd almost made love, she'd despaired that Blake would ever open up to her. He'd locked himself so tight behind his rules of control that she doubted he would ever trust her. She'd feared she wasn't the woman who could free that special, wondrously loving man.

Over the next few minutes he did open up, but not about anything she was expecting. He pushed up off the couch almost as fast as he'd sat down, shoved his hands into his pockets and paced around as he regaled her with a story about a newborn patient. It seemed that someone had come to his office—he wouldn't tell her the name—who'd asked him to keep a confidence, even though he should have taken the information to the law. There was a baby involved and a missing person.

Serena couldn't comprehend what he was really trying to tell her. She heard the story about the baby, but it seemed as if Blake were trying to own up to something and she couldn't fathom what it was. "Okay, so you met this man who was in some kind of trouble. In fact, the whole thing was so mysterious and weird that you were afraid he was in some kind of serious trouble..."

"Yes."

"But you had enough time with him to evaluate what kind of character he had. And trouble or not, he seemed like a good guy and a caring father to you..."

"Yeah. I'm sure of that. I can't explain it," Blake admitted. "It's not like I could come up with proof in a court of law."

"Well, this isn't a court of law. You're talking to me. If you think this guy is a good man, then he is. But more to the point, why are you so troubled about this? You're a doctor. This is your job every day. Not just listening to what people say, but making judgments based on how they act. Really, that's how you save people's lives. So you made some judgment calls about this man. I don't have any doubt at all that you're right about him, Blake, so what's the problem?"

She could have sworn she sounded patient and empathetic and caring, but he abruptly pivoted around and threw up his hands. "Serena, you're driving me nuts!"

"Huh?"

"I'm trying to be honest with you."

"And I swear I'm listening, Blake. But all I'm hearing is you confessing to some nonexistent crime."

"I should have reported the information about the birth and the missing person. To do less is going outside the law."

"And that's wonderful," Serena murmured.

"Wonderful?" His eyes shot skyward as if begging for some strength. "I'm trying to warn you about what kind of man I am. I'm not doing good with Nate, you know that. I keep screwing up. And you were talking the other night about this strange joy thing. I don't know that I ever had that joy thing, Serena. And then there are things like this. Nothing I'm doing lately seems to be right. Things I used to think were wrong seem right. I'm afraid I could talk myself into believing that I could be with you, with Nate, unless you take the reins and call a halt.''

"So you think telling me that whole story about how you handled this troubled man could make some kind of difference to me?''

"Not exactly. But maybe. It wasn't the man and the baby. It was that I'm trying to be honest with you about the kind of mistakes I've made and keep on making.''

"Whew. I'm really glad we talked about this,'' she murmured, and surged up from the couch. She walked closer to him.

And then she pounced.

# Nine

Damn woman was doing it again.

Kissing him. Rewarding him for doing something wrong. He'd been trying to warn her that he just wasn't the kind of man she needed in her life, for Pete's sake.

"Serena—"

"You were so darling. The way you picked up Nate and hugged him even when he was all covered with mud."

"Darling. Um. Thank you. I think." She smelled like sandalwood and peaches. Peaches from her shampoo, sandalwood and some other exotic flower from the scent on her skin. The scents were addling his wits. "But—"

"I had such a terrible day until you came over."

Apparently she thought he deserved another kiss for that. Only the taste of her was more madness. Sweet and exotic and alluring. "Thank you again. But—"

"There was nothing wrong. It was just one of those mean days. I was upset over the way we'd left each other last time, and feeling weird about Nate's first day of school, but mostly it was just me. One of those days when you trip over your own feet. And then you came in, and I saw the way you looked at Nate and it was like the sun filled my heart. Life's a risk, Blake, did you know that?''

Okay. Apparently she expected him to think while her bare hands were slowly chasing the shirt up his chest and over his head, her mouth coming back down on his with the smoothness of a hummingbird's landing. He wasn't thinking. He wasn't listening. His veins were pumping lots of rich, oxygen-rich blood, but all of it was pooling below his waist. ''Uh, I don't know as I have my mind on philosophy right at this precise moment.''

''Life is a risk. And love is an adventure. Can you try to believe me, Doc? It's okay if you sometimes let go and don't do everything by the rules.''

Considering her palms had ventured inside his pants and were slowly peeling them off, he was a little offended that she seemed to be suggesting he was not one to throw caution to the winds. He'd thrown his entire sanity to the winds. His head was buzzing. ''I believe in the rules, Serena. I know being into rules isn't fun. But I don't think it's a loving thing to be careless with someone else's heart or body or feelings.''

''You are so good.'' His pants fell to the floor. Her tongue swirled a sashaying pattern on his throat, hemming the edge of his jaw. Being a doctor, he was conscious of his blood pressure and that his had passed stroke level several minutes back. "But you aren't careless, Blake. You'd never deliberately hurt anyone. For that matter, you only get obsessed with the rules when they're about fathers."

"Oh, yeah?" He decided it was time for some revenge. First to go was the thin linen top she wore. As he skimmed it over her head, the few pins that had been holding her hair up loosened and her hair tumbled down, as lustrous as liquid ebony in the lamplight. He kissed her until he couldn't breathe. He kissed her until the heat and throbbing below his waist ached in pain. He kissed her until they were both gasping for air, any air. But apparently the kiss didn't have quite the same effect on her because she started talking again.

"Fathers are a touchy subject for you, love, which is so understandable. You started out with a dad who wouldn't give you a word of praise for love or money. It had to feel like relief when you first realized there was a reason, that he wasn't really your father, only then it turned out that your real dad was a philanderer without a conscience in sight. So you were crushed twice by fathers. Terribly."

"Um, Serena, if you want to talk dirty to me, it's okay. But I have to tell you honestly that I haven't heard a word you said since you stripped off my clothes." And he hers. Not that she was completely naked yet, but she was close. Her linen top had fit so loosely that he hadn't been sure if she was wearing a bra. Now he knew. She wasn't. Her nipples were dusky in the lamplight, the top of her breasts golden and smooth and firm, the weight of them a heavy, erotic heartbeat in his palm. A finger grazing the tip made her breath catch and a flush whisper up her throat and darken her eyes.

"I'm going to say this, Blake, and I'm not going to let you distract me. At some level I know you're listening. You keep trying to make up for that background. Those two less-than-stellar dads. Those dads who hurt you. The thing you don't see is that you rose above them both eons ago. You're better than both those men. You were better than them before you were out of diapers."

Her lecture was very nice. Or he was pretty sure it would be, if he'd been paying attention. What he was paying attention to, with intense concentration, was her skimming off the rest of her clothes and his. Her lifting her arms, coming to him, naked to his naked, her smooth, warm golden skin to his hair-roughened textures, her nurturing lips to his hungry, lonesome ones. That feeling of wicked was coming on him. That same feeling of wicked, wanton immersion he always felt around her. He made one last desperate attempt at sanity.

"Serena, I didn't bring any protection."

Her palms framed his face, making her his world, his only world; her eyes were liquid fire the way she looked at him. "You can't do it, Blake. You can't close yourself off forever, afraid of making a mistake, worrying that you're like either of your fathers.

You're not. But you have to want to risk. You and I can never work unless you're willing to reach out and take that risk. I can't do it alone, can you understand?''

What he understood was that she could talk all night. He was through talking. He'd had nothing to say from the instant she'd started peeling off clothes and his hormones had shrieked a fire-alarm message that she was willing. More than willing. That she was inviting them to make love. Damn. Mere seconds before, he'd been worried about the ethical reasons why this wasn't right.

But he touched her and all that went away.

This was a good idea.

A great idea.

This was the best idea he'd had in his entire adult life. No one made him "feel" like Serena. Ever had, ever would, ever could. Any problem or risk was worth it when he was with her. Life was bigger, brighter, bolder, ecstatically worth living. Yes, that familiar wild, wicked feeling made him feel guilty, made him worry, too. But, man—worry had never tasted as much fun as this before.

She gave so willingly, so warmly. The lick of her tongue inspired the sweep of his hand. Her skin heated for him, turned slick for him. Her breasts ignited, tightened, reacting to his hands, his mouth.

He lifted her, not having any clear destination in mind, but knowing they had to move. If Nate woke up, he mustn't find them running around the living room naked. Serena noosed her arms around his neck, whispering kisses on his throat and ear, providing no help to the navigational crisis in any way. His thigh bumped a corner. He kept moving. Away from lights. Down the hall. Five kisses later, to the end of the hall. Her room.

There were no lights on in her room. It wasn't midnight-dark yet, but the shadows were as thick as a charcoal fog, so initially he couldn't make out any shapes. What he could do was slide her down his body so that she was standing on her feet again. Then close the door. Quietly. And latch it. Deliberately. Then lay her up against that door and kiss her good. Kiss her hard. Kiss her senseless.

Kiss her in a way that tactfully communicated that all bets were off. It was too late to climb back into the plane; this sky dive was already in motion. Blood was already soaring through his veins, excitement hustling through his pulse, the rush of needing her pounding in his ears. He remembered being married, remembered loving sex his whole life, but never the way it'd been with her seven years ago…and now. This strange, alien feeling of freedom. A loosening from the inside out, because he didn't have a choice but to give and give up everything he had. With her. For her.

"Bed," she whispered. "Hurry."

"Where?" Even though his pupils had dilated, he saw no mattress.

"Chinese bed. There in the wall."

He had no clue what a Chinese bed was, but she slipped away from him and lit a candle, a small one, just a pool of vanilla scent in a bowl, but the flame was enough to provide illumination. Even if he hadn't had the motivation, he could have figured out the Chinese bed thing. The full-size mattress was built into the wall, the bed itself concealed behind draperies, filmy folds of drapery that allowed light, yet still provided complete privacy.

"I've never seen a bed like this." He really wasn't up for making conversation. The bed was just so unusual, and it was obviously going to be part of their lovemaking. At some instinctive level he just wanted to know why she'd picked it, and what it meant to her.

"You like it?" she asked.

"I'd like any bed with you in it."

Her smile was a flash of sassy white teeth, and alluring with promise. "The Chinese are like my Cheyenne. The women are modest. They only want to show themselves to the man they love."

And then she clasped his hand and, pushing aside the filmy draperies, pulled him inside to the concealing feminine nest of a bed. He caught the scents of sandalwood and sage and night-blooming jasmine. None were as exotic or arousing as the scent coming off her skin.

She was so breathtaking. Her flesh was smooth and golden, her body so sleek and supple. Fluid as water, more sensuous than silk, her arms and legs wound around him, pulling him down, pulling him in. He saw her eyes, liquid with emotion, inhaled her lips in a kiss that threatened to drown them both in a deep, dark current. Need bubbled up, turned into a craving that sparked fire deep in his belly.

He had to have her—sexually, but so much more than sexually. At that instant he feared he'd never recover if he didn't make love to her, right then, that moment, no later. A crazy fear rose inside him like a devil fear. Some strange instinct that he could lose her—lose anything that ever mattered to him—if he failed to make her part of his life.

She sucked in a breath, her spine arching, when he filled her, fast, hard, completely. He wanted to woo her, wile and beguile her, yet the urgency gave him no choice. He had to hurry to make sure she didn't go anywhere, hurry to make sure that nothing could happen before he had her, that nothing could break this priceless magic spell…

And then there was no spell. There was just him and her in the most earthy and natural of ways. The mattress was softer than earth, her pillows softer than sky. The glowing candle barely cut the darkness, yet he could still see the light in her eyes, the light coming off her like rays of emotion into him. Love. For the first time in his life he really felt it. For the first time in his life, he felt as though he belonged somewhere, to someone, and he wasn't alone.

They came together with the fury of a thunderstorm and the drenching sweetness of a spring rain. Afterward, he sank into her, wanting to stay joined with her through the whole night, but of course, he couldn't. Eventually he got up, took care of business, and then just eased down beside her again, sharing the same pillow, holding her, wrapped around her, warm and close.

He thought she'd fallen asleep, yet when her eyes finally opened, his were waiting for her. He could have studied her for an eternity, not just her face, but every gorgeous bone, every millimeter of smooth golden skin. Her mouth had a wine blush from his kisses, her hair fell in a tangled waterfall. He thought that in a minute he'd get up and brush it. Just to do something for her that no one else had ever done.

Instead he stroked her back, from her nape down the skimming slope of her spine to her fanny, then over again. He tried to remember the woman he'd married and divorced. Tried to remember his growing-up years, the crushing wait of always trying to please his dad, always failing. Tried to remember medical school. Tried to remember Garrett first telling him that he was a Kincaid. They were all big memories in his life, inexorable parts of who he was, yet nothing would stick in his mind.

Nothing of the past mattered. Only now mattered. Only Serena. And for some reason, the only mirror-clear memory in his mind was making love with her, that one time, seven years ago. He'd been grieving over the loss of his mom, feeling lower than a pit about himself and his life, and when Serena made love with him, it'd been like a dazzling white light at the bleakest hour of his life. At the time he'd thought it'd been some kind of apparition, a fluke, something that just seemed so perfect because the rest of his life had been so dark right then.

He hadn't realized it was Serena.

That she was the white light. It had never been the incredible sex, or a measure of the good or bad times in his life. It was about her. How wonderful she was. How special. And how differently he felt about himself when he was with her.

From nowhere he felt her fingertips graze his jaw, in the tenderest of caresses. He closed his eyes, inhaling the sensation. "I know, brown eyes. I have to go."

"No, you don't."

"I mean before Nate gets up. I haven't forgotten that it's his first day of school tomorrow. And even if the two of you didn't have an extra-big day, you wouldn't want him to find me here when he wakes up. It wouldn't be right. But I really don't want to leave you right now, Serena."

"And I don't want you to get up. To leave at all." Softly then, "I love you, Blake."

"I love you, too." He meant it. But as he cuddled Serena close again, he wasn't positive what she meant by the same words. People said things in the dark and in the wonder of passion. Hell, he was thirty-two-years old and just figuring out that she was everything.

Later, though, when Blake finally forced himself to get up, he looked around her bedroom as he quietly pulled on his clothes. He'd never been in here before. She had things of all kinds from all over the world, not expensive artsy stuff so much as ideas and textures and colors from all kinds of cultures. Fascinating, just like her. But as he silently dug into his back pocket for keys, he thought of his gray apartment and the place he used to have in L.A. that had a lot of chrome and black—expensive chrome and black, but still, essentially colorless.

As he walked out into the night, qualms started scraping on his nerves. He wasn't sure if he fit in. She fit for him, but whether Serena needed him for anything, wanted him for anything, was still a huge, troubling question in his mind. If he couldn't add something to her life—and Nate's—he had no business being with her.

Serena was nonstop busy the whole next day, but by three-thirty she was more antsy than a wet cat. Her kids had been wonderful. Fourth hour was probably going to be the blinger—there was always one class that caused more trouble than others. And first hour, she had a couple kids that looked over-tired, white-eyed—something in their families wasn't going right, even if Serena had no idea what it was yet. Fifth hour was a teacher's dream—the kids all cared, all loved science, actually listened to her. A miracle on the first day of school, as any high school teacher knew.

It wasn't just her first day of the school year, of course. And even while she was memorizing names and intuiting the personality of each class, all day she found herself meandering to the far windows in her science room.

The Whitehorn grade school and high school were in different buildings, separated by a giant multipurpose sports field. The whole school complex, including the administration center, was smack-dab in the middle of town, but protected from traffic in a cul de sac. From Serena's classroom windows, she could see the rooftops of the police and fire stations. More relevant, she could look across the soccer field directly over to the first grade classroom—Nate's classroom.

At lunch, Blake had called and managed to reach her in the teachers' lounge. "Hey, love."

The endearment had made her insides feel like a fresh toasted marshmallow. How was she supposed to think after a hello like that? She murmured, "Hi, you," but she thought, "Hi, lover."

"Do you have any report on how our son is surviving his first day of school yet?"

"No report, but my free hour is second hour, and I ran over there to spy. He seemed happy."

"Do you like his teacher?"

"Well, no," Serena admitted.

"What's this no? There's something wrong with her?"

She chuckled. "No, absolutely nothing. Her name

is Mrs. Harvey. Parents love her, the kids love her, and, until our son got in that class, I did, too.''

''Ah. You don't think she'll appreciate our Nate?''

''Not like I want someone to appreciate our son. You know. I want his teacher to think he's the most special child she ever had. Heads above every child she's ever met or taught. Fascinating to her from every aspect. I want her to be tolerant of every slight fault, astounded with his brilliance.''

''Well, yeah. So what's your point? Even a moron of a teacher could figure that stuff about our son five minutes after meeting him.''

Oh, God. Blake was going to be worse than her.

The memory of his call stayed with her through the rest of the school day. But at the three-thirty bell, she left her purse and papers and chased across the soccer field almost faster than the speed of sound—no different from every other first-grade mom who hovered anxiously at the door for her baby to come out.

And there he was, loping toward her. Shirt untucked, shoes untied, something red on his favorite T-shirt. ''Hey, Mom!''

''Hey, slugger.'' She'd been a teacher too long. She knew perfectly well that she couldn't grab him in front of his peers, but her baby already looked three years older in just six short hours. All she really wanted to do was kiss and hug him, and then stuff him back into the womb where he'd be safe from life's hurts forever. She settled for ruffling his hair and asking casually, ''So, how'd it go?''

"Okay. But I'm starving. In fact I'm so starving that I'm about to die. Can we go home?"

"We sure can. I have to stop by my classroom to get my purse—and I want you to know how to get there, too, sweetie. But that'll only take a few seconds. How'd you like to stop at the Hip Hop Café for an ice cream before going home?"

Hunched over a booth, lapping up some ungodly-flavored turquoise ice cream, he spilled out the whole story of the day. "Mrs. Harvey likes me. I can read. You wouldn't believe it, Mom, but most of the kids can't. And they don't know how to use a computer, either. So I get to help the other kids sometimes. Scott Middleton took Janey Smith's pencil off her desk, though. Just took it. Just like that. It wasn't his."

"Did Mrs. Harvey see him do it?"

"Yeah, she saw. Only Scott lied and said the pencil was his. And then there's this girl named Elizabeth who wouldn't let me alone. I mean, we're talking major issues there."

"Major issues, huh? Where on earth did you hear that term?" She reached for a napkin, her son's fifth. Nate may be precocious enough to pick up terms such as "major issues," but he was still young enough to make gigantic messes with an ice-cream cone.

"I think this school thing's gonna be easy. Recess was fun. And if you get your work done, then you can be on the computer more."

"That sounds cool."

"Uh-huh. I was afraid the whole deal was gonna

be boring, but it's not so bad. I was gonna tell Dr. Blake about it."

"Well, something tells me he'll be anxious to hear what you thought of school, so he'll probably stop over tonight."

"Yeah, that's what I thought. Mom?" Nate lifted his face for another napkin wipe. "How come Dr. Blake comes over all the time?"

Serena's pulse skipped a beat. "Do you have a problem with him coming over so much?"

"No. He's okay. It's not that. It's that I don't get it."

"You don't get what exactly?"

"We have lots of friends over. But it just isn't the same as when Dr. Blake comes over. For one thing, you're kissing him all the time. Mom?"

"Uh, what?"

"I think kissing is gross. You like doing it, fine. But I'm never doing it with a girl, no way."

"You might change your mind," Serena suggested.

"I'm never changing my mind." He motioned emphatically, shaking drips of turquoise ice cream all over the tabletop. "I'm telling you, all girls have issues. And do you know what their main issue is?"

She stifled a laugh. "No, Nate, I have no idea. But you sure learned a lot in first grade today."

"I did," he agreed. "Elizabeth was the one who 'splained about the issues. Anyway, they're not boys. That's what their main issue is. That they're stuck being girls. Except for you, Mom. You're okay."

"I'm relieved that you think so," Serena said dryly. "So you got all this from this girl named Elizabeth, huh?"

"Some of it. But some of it— Do you know Gloria Rivertree?"

"No, hon."

"Well, she's in my class." Nate referred to this as if he'd been in school for years. "Her mom and dad split up awhile ago. Then her mom had some guys over. They were kissing all the time. Gloria thought she and her sister were going to get a new dad, but you'd have to know her. She's pretty dumb, Mom. Even I know you don't get a dad because of kissing. There's other stuff that matters."

Serena carefully picked her jaw up off the floor. "Oh? What do you think that other stuff is?"

"Well, like, dads have to have jobs. And I think they have to have some money, too. Don't ask me any more questions, okay? I've been thinking all day. I need a rest from thinking now. Did I tell you that I got to erase the blackboard?"

"No, you didn't."

"It's because I could read. You get to do a lot more things in life if you can read."

On the drive home, Serena wished Blake could have heard the whole conversation. Her heart kept charging the same spark plug: he belonged here. With her. With his son. With the three of them free to be the family they really were.

Yet her mood had turned sober by the time they

pulled into the drive and Whiskey and the cats bounded out with lonesome barks and purrs to greet them. Once Nate started asking questions, Serena had always known that she and Blake would have to make some immediate decisions. She'd wanted the two to get to know each other before springing the news on Nate about Blake's real relationship to him. But that was never supposed to be forever. They'd spent time together now. It was past time she came clean with her son.

Only she'd spent the same time falling so hard in love with Blake again that she wasn't sure she could recover this time if he didn't return her feelings.

He cared about her, she knew. And he'd used that precious "love" word last night. But whether his feelings for her were still driven primarily by responsibility, Serena still felt unsure. Suddenly she felt the pressure of a knife pressing against her heart.

No affair between them could last long. She was unwilling to sleep with a man she wasn't married to, not with a son as aware and bright as Nate was. She loved Blake. She'd willingly made love with him, and she'd started out willingly risking all she was in the hope they might build something together. What other choice was there? You had to be willing to risk it all to have anything worthwhile.

Only Serena couldn't stop thinking that time was not just running out on the two of them. It had run out. Nate had started asking questions. She and Blake needed to decide, immediately, what they wanted to do together—for him, and for them.

Serena was a willing risk taker. Always had been, always would be. Only the stakes in this particular heart game were losing Blake. Forever, this time.

# Ten

Blake stood in the center of his living room, a rag hanging from his hand.

Serena was coming over in a few minutes. She'd called, saying that she really needed to talk with him. Rather than work himself into an ulcer of worry, he figured he should do something industrious until she got here, like dust.

Only a little belatedly he recognized that there was nothing to dust. Even after all these weeks, there was nothing in the place but some patchy rental furniture. Hell. He had the money to make the place into something. He just hadn't put up a picture or added anything personal because he hadn't given a damn. Also, when he'd first come back to Whitehorn, he'd had no idea how long he was going to stay.

Still didn't.

The difference between spring and now, though, was that, for the first time in his life, Blake knew where he wanted his home to be. What he didn't know was whether Serena wanted him in her life.

At the sound of a knock on his back door, he jumped as if a dragon had stepped on his shadow.

"Come on in!" Swiftly he flicked the rag over the only lampshade in the room—maybe that made it look cleaner?—and then hurriedly pushed the dust rag under a couch cushion and jogged toward the kitchen door.

His heart deflated instantly. He'd just assumed it was Serena. But instead of the woman who was causing him a regular heart attack, a man stepped inside. Blake had to scrape his brain before the name would come to him. Adam. Adam Benson.

"Blake. I only have a minute, and if you're busy, I can disappear again. I happened to be in town for dinner and it started to bother me that the two of us hadn't spent more than five seconds together since the Kincaid picnic."

"Adam, I'm glad you stopped." Blake shot out a hand, musing that remembering his own half brother's name should hardly be such a big deal. But, of course, all of Larry Kincaid's bastards were in the same boat, and hadn't known each other existed until a few months ago. "I am expecting company, a friend, but come on in and sit down for a while. Let me get you a drink. You have a favorite poison?"

"Nothing alcoholic, although I wouldn't mind coffee if you had some around. I still have a long drive ahead. And truthfully, I cut out of the Hip Hop Café before I'd had dessert or coffee because the place was so crazy tonight."

"Yeah?" Blake started some cappuccino brewing—enough in case Serena wanted some, too—and then motioned Adam into the living room. He really didn't want Adam to stay or to get too comfortable. All he wanted was time alone with the woman who was slowly but surely driving him insane. Yet Adam was one of his new family members for whom he'd felt a compatibility from their first meeting.

They looked alike, for one thing. Adam stretched out his long legs, his height and jet-black hair similar to Blake's. The gray eyes were different, and there was harshness engrained in Adam's expression. Yet the man had a toughness of character that Blake admired, and a loneliness he exuded that Blake instinctively related to.

Initially Adam had hardly come across as friendly, he seemed withdrawn when they first met, as if he wanted nothing to do with the Kincaids. Perhaps he sensed that Blake felt the same wariness, because the two men had seemed to find themselves standing together more than once, testing out a conversation, checking out each other's character.

Blake was unsure that anyone would call their relationship a friendship yet, but Adam had taken to occasionally stopping by. They'd both shared information about their backgrounds.

Adam was thirty-seven, five years older than Blake, and also the first of Larry Kincaid's bastards. When Larry had seduced Adam's mom, she'd been an innocent teenager, in no position to support a child. She'd turned to her older sister for help, and it was that aunt and uncle who'd raised Adam, even though it was tough supporting him on a domestic and a ranch hand's wages. Adam grew up feeling loved in a way that Blake had never felt, but the two men still shared strong common ground. They both knew what it was to have mothers who'd made desperate decisions to cope with an unexpected pregnancy—and what having an irresponsible creep for a blood father had done to their lives.

Blake remembered Adam's story, but his mind was so much on Serena's coming visit that he wasn't really listening to Adam's conversation. Something was obviously troubling him. He was talking about one of the local families, the Rutherfords, with fire in his eyes and ice in his voice.

Blake tried to catch up without letting on he'd lost the conversational thread. "I remember you saying something about Victoria Rutherford before. She was your first love in high school, right?"

"Until she threw me over. But it was her dad who fired my uncle Dan—Dan Benson—and like I told you, Dan was the only dad I ever knew and ranch work was all Dan ever knew how to do. I'll tell you I don't like holding a grudge, but I have no use for the Rutherfords. The financial trouble they've got on their ranch right now feels like revenge. What I found out when I was having dinner…"

When Blake heard another knock, he immediately bolted to his feet. Truthfully, he was confused why Adam was telling him all this stuff about the Rutherford family. It wasn't as if Blake knew them himself. But he tried to snap more alert when Adam started talking about revenge. Maybe the two men didn't know each other well enough to be close, but Blake had never seen revenge work out.

This just wasn't a time he could possibly talk to Adam, though, and once he opened the door, any prayer he had of concentrating disappeared like smoke.

His lover's face was waiting for him with one of those smiles that was just for him. Her hair was brushed smooth, let loose for once, and shimmered down her back in a long raven fall. Her brown eyes were a pure liquid topaz and her clothes nothing fancy—they never were—but the loose linen tunic and slacks modestly draped her lush breasts and rounded hips. Modest had always seemed to be her nature, yet the way she moved toward him was as dangerous and sensual as a wicked temptress. Or maybe he thought that because he seemed to hopelessly respond to her that way.

"Hi," she murmured, her lips already tilting.

His were already dipping down. The hello kiss invoked more hopeless, helpless cataclysmic feelings in him. He could have stopped breathing before stopping himself from touching her, no matter how much was unresolved between them. But she realized swiftly that they weren't alone when Adam cleared his throat.

Within a few minutes she was introduced to Adam and was curled up in the dove-gray chair, nursing a cappuccino. She never gave any hint that she wasn't just dropping by to see a casual friend, much less that she wasn't completely comfortable with Adam's unexpected presence.

"Adam just stopped by for a few minutes after having dinner at the Hip Hop Café," Blake explained.

"Best place for gossip in the state," Serena said dryly.

Hoping to establish some common ground between Adam and Serena, Blake added, "I understand one of the things being talked about tonight was something about the Rutherfords."

"The Rutherfords?" Serena turned directly to Adam. "I went to college at the same time as Victoria. We've been good friends for years."

Adam flashed a sharp, meaningful glance at Blake, as if asking him not to say anything further about their previous conversation. Blake hesitated, feeling confused, unable to understand why Adam wouldn't want to pursue the subject of the Rutherfords with Serena. She was the one person who could probably give him direct information, since she knew the family. She might even be able to clear up whatever Adam's problem was with them.

Still, there was no chance for Blake to pursue anything further about the Rutherfords, because Adam promptly went on a humorous venting binge about being unable to eat at the Hip Hop without a dose of gossip and sensationalism. "And I'll tell you, the place was really buzzing tonight. All about that Christina Montgomery disappearance."

"Oh! I haven't heard anything in days. Did they finally find her?" Serena asked.

"No. That's the whole problem. The cops are involved in the search now. And the mayor being her dad, naturally Ellis is raising hell. I gather her older sister—Rachel, is it?—just flew in from Chicago."

"I used to know Rachel, but I haven't seen her in years now," Serena said thoughtfully. "Once she left for college, she almost made a point of not coming home. I always had the feeling that she didn't get along with her dad any more than Christina did."

"I don't know. I just know that she's back now, specifically because she's determined to find out where Christina is, come hell or high water. As far as I can tell, there's no particular reason to assume anything bad happened to the girl. She could have just run away."

Serena nodded. "She wasn't happy at home, that's for sure. Not since her mom died."

"Yeah, well. That's what folks were saying at the Hip Hop. Everyone was speculating about what man she was involved with, only then this woman came into the restaurant. Winona Cobbs. Do you know her?"

"You can't live in Whitehorn without knowing Winona," Serena said with a chuckle. "Even if every woman in town didn't occasionally sucker into her Stop-n-Swap store, Winona's our town psychic."

Adam and Blake both stared at her, then each other. "How do women know this stuff?" And then Adam added, "Believe me, she was dressed the part. Long, goofy dress, beads and crystals hanging all over the place. Anyway, she comes into the restaurant, touches the scarf that I guess belonged to the missing girl, and immediately claims that she can 'hear' Christina screaming in pain. Like anyone's going to believe this?"

"Somehow I suspect that everyone in the Hip Hop believed it," Serena said.

"They did." Adam threw up his hands. "And that got everyone in the Hip Hop buzzing double-time. They figured if she was in pain, then maybe she was in labor—because the whole town had figured out that she was pregnant, even if her daddy kept denying it. Maybe she was growing a watermelon in her stomach, who knows? Whatever, not like the woman is any of my business." He stood, looked at both of them. "Serena, it was wonderful to meet you. But you should have kicked me out before this. I've shot enough bull, really just wanted to say hello to Blake, see how he was doing. Now, though, I'll get out of both your hair."

He was gone faster than two shakes of a lamb's tail. When Blake came back from the door, Serena was taking a last sip of cappuccino and studying his face over the cup rim. "Are all of your new Kincaid brothers like that?"

"Well, everyone isn't in town. But it's pretty interesting, how easily we all started talking together. Even if we never realized that we were related before, it seems we all had similar experiences growing up. Or, let's say, we all developed similar ideas about responsibility from having such an irresponsible father. So it made it easier to feel a kinship from the beginning.''

She nodded. ''Adam seems nice. Maybe the exterior is a little austere? But it was obvious he was trying to be warm and friendly, and besides that, there's just something in the eyes that says 'good man.''' Without waiting for him to comment, she suddenly switched subjects. ''That's what you were talking about the other night, wasn't it?''

''Beg your pardon?''

''The story you told me about the man who showed up in the middle of the night, asking you for help and to keep quiet about his coming to you. The problem was about Christina, wasn't it? And her baby. It all started to click in my mind when Adam mentioned the newest gossip in town.''

Blake hesitated.

''It's okay, Blake. You don't have to answer. I know you gave your word and I'm really not asking for the particulars.'' She stood. ''I just wanted to say, try to trust your own judgment, okay? God knows, I trust you. Forget the law. Forget what anyone else would think or say. Just let your heart talk to you, just this once.''

Her perception startled him, though it shouldn't have. Her intuitiveness had always seen straight into his soul. ''Yeah, well, my heart told me that the man

involved was a good father. But all the evidence—
everything I knew about the facts—led me to think
there was something seriously wrong and I should be
more suspicious.'' Just as his circumstances with her,
Blake had long realized. No matter how much he
wanted to be with her and Nate, he'd been afraid that
his heart was creating excuses to do something that
he wanted, instead of being sure it was right for her.

She carted her empty mug into the kitchen, then
came out, but only as far as the doorway. ''How many
times have you heard the facts on the news that didn't
turn out to be the real story? Facts don't always lead
you to the truth. Just once I wish you'd try listening
to your heart and believing what you feel.''

She was trying to tell him something meaningful,
Blake understood, because he saw the woman's look
and he saw her eyes. Something really mattered to
her. Something she was trying to tell him. But he just
couldn't be one of those modern guys who spilled out
feelings like a flushed-open water faucet. He'd come
from two fathers who'd managed to tear up his life
by making uncaring, irresponsible choices instead of
honorable ones. He didn't want to be like them and
he didn't want any more mistakes. Not with her.
''You're hovering by the door,'' he said uneasily.

''Yeah. Nate's over at his uncle Wolf's but not for
overnight. I can't stay more than a few more minutes.
There was just something I wanted to tell you in private.'' She offered him a smile then, softer than
sunshine. ''Nate started asking questions about you.

Personal questions, about you and me. I could hold him off if I had to…but really, don't you think it's time to tell him you're his dad? Would you like to do it together?''

Blake sank to the edge of the armchair, feeling as if the oomph had been knocked out of him. ''Serena…'' God, he'd been waiting for this, hoping for this. ''You know I wasn't going to bring it up unless you volunteered that telling him was the right thing to do.''

''Well, I think it is the right thing. In fact, I think waiting longer would be a mistake. He's noticed how often you're around. He's accepted you. And that's why we were waiting, wasn't it? To help him feel comfortable with you, so you weren't a stranger?''

''That was part of it. But not all.'' He gestured. ''Serena, I wanted to earn a place in his life. So he never felt like he had to accept me just because of having a blood relationship.''

''Yes, I understand that, Blake, always did. But don't you think that's water way under the bridge? He enjoys being with you.''

Blake wasn't so sure. ''I'll tell you what. Could I take him—if he wants to go—for an overnight with me? Like…camping. Tent camping. Something I know he likes to do, but just with the two of us?''

''Well, sure, I think that's a great idea.'' She hesitated. ''But if you're thinking to use that private time to tell him—''

''No, Serena. I wouldn't do that. You're the one

who's always been in his life. Whenever he finds out, I think you should be there and be the one to tell him. I'd just like one night alone with him. If he's willing to go. Nothing I've tried with him has gone right so far—''

"Blake! Nothing's gone that terribly wrong!"

Her memories and his were remarkably different. Blake remembered a volcano blowing up all over her kitchen, a kite crashing on its own, a computer game that humiliated the kid to play with him because he was so bad, buying him the wrong toy...

Blake scraped a hand through his hair. The list just went on and on. He didn't want to think about it. He didn't need to mentally relist those failures to be aware that he'd failed to prove himself in Nate's eyes. "Just let me take him for an overnight camping trip, okay? And then we'll talk about this again."

Serena frowned. "Blake, I don't know what's on your mind. But if somehow you thought I was talking about marriage—as in, that I think you and I have to pin down our relationship for Nate in absolute terms—I wasn't. I swear I wasn't. I just think it's time Nate knows who you are. I think it'd be good for him, and good for you. Your father/son relationship is not about me."

"Everything in his life is about you, Serena. You're not separable from your son. Do you think I don't know that?" Blake hesitated again. The air was getting thick and murky with all their careful words and too many things that weren't being said. "You wouldn't even consider marriage?"

"I never said that."

Hell, he was scared to press her, but even more scared not to. "But you brought up the marriage word, brown eyes. And in the context of not mentioning that word to Nate, which implies to me that it's not something you want our son to believe could happen."

Her eyes hadn't left his, but now her hand reached for him. Fingertips grazed his arm, just a touch-me gesture, the sparest of physical contacts, yet the touch of her felt as intimate as the softness in her eyes. "I know I've told you this before," she said quietly. "But when my parents died, a white couple took in my brothers and me, kept our family together. They were so wonderful to us, but Blake, it was part of my whole childhood...knowing that they'd personally turned their whole lives upside down to take us in. I loved them. They taught me to see the positive in the hardest times, to find something in the wildest storm. But—"

"But..." He had no idea how her foster parents had gotten into this conversation.

"But they never had a spare dime. And taking in three kids was a terrible struggle for them, just to meet basic needs. Every day of my childhood, I felt beholden. No matter how much I loved them, I always felt like a responsibility. And I just can't do that ever again in my life. I know you feel responsible for

Nate—and me. But I don't want you to offer marriage, ever, because of feeling any kind of obligation.''

''I understand.''

The hell he did, Serena thought. He understood nothing. A tidal wave of love, fierce and compelling, swept through her heart and blinded her to everything else at that moment. He thought marrying her was the right thing, for Nate's sake. No different than he'd have offered marriage years before, if she'd told him she was pregnant.

But she wanted love or nothing.

Every woman on the planet wanted a responsible man. But she wasn't other women, and she couldn't survive again always feeling beholden, always feeling like someone's responsibility. She needed Blake to care what she needed and either take the risk, or let her go.

Maybe he heard her this time.

Maybe he really did understand.

Because he swooped her up into his arms faster than a devil fire and he kissed her first, instead of the other way around. She needed to get home for Nate. It wasn't that late, and she knew he was perfectly content at her brother's, but she'd told him what time she would pick him up and Serena had always kept her word.

But, oh, man. Right then, time didn't seem very important. Right then, in fact there seemed to be no time, no gravity. No gray-drab room that sang of Blake's loneliness, no clock ticking in his kitchen, no car lights flashing through his blinds from passing traffic. There was just him and her and a kiss that sucked her in faster than the speed of light.

Tastes and scents crashed into each other, familiar now, the way you knew the beat of a rock-and-roll song from the first notes and couldn't help but start moving to it. His taste had always moved her, his textures and scents had always revved her personal drums to dark, low, hot rhythms. The feel of his hands on her skin, in her hair, the way his gaze fastened hot and bright on her face made her feel as if she was all that existed in his universe.

They'd been talking about Nate. About telling him about Blake being his dad. About their pasts. About marriage. How a kiss frenzied enough to shake the rafters came from all that, she didn't know or care. Her heart just kept whispering to go with it. Reward Blake for giving in to an impulse. Show him that risk didn't have to be scary because loving someone was the only thing that made huge risks worth taking.

*See what we are,* her heart cried to him. Because in her head she knew that time was running out. She couldn't sleep with Blake for long because of Nate. But so much more to the point, she couldn't force Blake to reach out for the kind of love she believed was worth fighting for. He either felt it or they had nothing.

But, oh, right then, they seemed to have it all.

Clothes stripped down, peeled away. Breaths shortened, rasped, turned into sighs and gasps. Skin heated, became slick and slippery. On the inside Serena could feel the building sensual power, heady and feminine, giving her the courage to try anything, do anything. For him. Only for Blake.

Urgent kisses only aroused more urgent kisses. For her, it was always the same. She'd never thought his being the father of her son was an accident. No, they hadn't planned Nate that long-ago night, but her feminine soul had chosen Blake. He was her natural alpha mate. The man who stirred her like none other, who had spoiled her for all others. No faults or problems mattered. Loving him enriched her life, made her more of who she wanted to be, made her hunger for him, only for him.

The ghastly gray carpet was scratchy and rough on her bare back. His place was so unlike her intimate private bedroom with its creative comforts and softness. Yet she wrapped her legs around him, pulling him down to her. Somehow a table leg tangled with his foot. The glare of a lamp bulb was in the wrong place, blinding them at the wrong time. A phone rang in the distance.

None of it mattered. None. She felt as if she were emptying her wallets in Vegas, risking all she had this time, giving him all she was. Either he understood the gift or they had nowhere to go. This time she felt his love as surely as if he'd bellowed the words at earsplitting volumes. His possession was swift, possessive, tender. Fierce tender. Wild tender. Love tender.

They surged toward completion faster than a runaway tidal wave, teasing each other, swelling and withdrawing, yet always pounding toward that ultimate goal. His whole body clenched when hers did. Passion sheened his eyes, as it did hers. And when she cried out his name in desperation, he hissed out hers, just as that wave tucked them under, sucked them under, swelled them into a crescendo of a climax.

Later, though, he laughed when he looked around in a daze and saw what they'd done to each other and the room. So did she. But when he bent his head to kiss her that last time—a lover's kiss—she sensed fear again. He'd shown her love without question. She didn't need the words. But now he was holding her again, as if he would responsibly protect her. Rather than if he wanted to.

And Serena was afraid that she'd lost him.

# Eleven

"Oh, boy! Oh, boy! This is cool, Dr. Blake!"

"You like it so far, huh?" Blake's heart swelled bigger than the Goodyear blimp. Nothing he'd done with Nate before had seemed to work out, but tonight he really had hopes. He couldn't ask Serena into his life until he was absolutely certain that Nate could love him. It'd never work. Not for Serena, and not for their son. So far, though—for the first time!—Nate seemed to be having an absolute blast with him.

"We get to put up the tent next, right?"

"You bet. It's too early to settle down, but once we get the tent put up, we'll have a place to hang out when we get tired."

"I'm not tired at all."

"I know you're not, sport."

"And we can have marshmallows for dinner, right? And I get to help you put up the tent? And then we're both going to explore the wild'rness? And there could even be bears and lynx and mountain lions and stuff?"

"Yes, I'm counting on you to help me put up the tent. You know, the real men's work. And then we'll explore all you want. Then we'll start a fire and make dinner, marshmallows included.''

"And there could be bears." Clearly Nate didn't want him to forget that important point.

"There could be bears," Blake echoed. Personally, though, he thought any wildlife would have to be mentally challenged to still be hanging around, considering how much noise the two humans had made tromping up here.

As he peeled off the bulky backpack, he gratefully rolled his shoulders to shake out the stiff kinks. But his gaze never left Nate.

He'd chosen Kincaid land for their overnight camping outing because he thought it might bring him luck and he hoped his son might develop a love and feeling of belonging for this stretch of land. It was a show-off kind of Saturday afternoon. A balmy seventy-five, even for September. They'd only had to hike in about a half hour to find a perfect spot. Gold light showered on the rolling hillside, catching the color of fall wildflowers. A bare breath of wind whistling through the treetops, and the pale blue sky stretched as big as a man's soul.

Or a boy's.

God. A wave of love washed through him as he watched his son scamper over rocks, pretending to be a frontier explorer. He'd always liked kids, but nothing—nothing—resembled the emotion that Nate stirred in him.

A wall of sunlight surrounded the boy. He glowed with confidence, the kind Blake had never had as a child. Nate was independent. Maybe a little too much so. He asked endless questions, had no end of curiosity about life, could sit and stare at an anthill for a half hour without moving, then suddenly roll in the yard with Whiskey and the kittens. He was smart and strong and good-looking, probably the handsomest boy that had been born in this decade, and for damn sure the smartest. Temporarily he was also filthy from head to toe. Hell, how could a kid get so dirty so fast? But his teeth were blinding white when he grinned, and God knew he smiled and laughed all the time.

Blake was hard-pressed not to dream. He wanted his son to meet Trent, and all the rest of his uncles, and Garrett Kincaid. Like a craving hunger, he wanted the chance to raise him and raise him right, not like the fathers Blake had had but like the father he'd wanted to have. Serena was already doing a fabulous job with him, but Blake wanted to do Men Things. Install honor and responsibility and justice. Not as if a mom couldn't teach the same values, but males just did certain things differently with other males. They taught each other a code. The Good Man code.

"Hey, Dr. Blake? What happens if we see a rattler?"

Run, Blake thought. "Well, I think if we make

enough noise, most snakes are going to stay out of our sight.''

"Because they're afraid, right? Because we're so big and strong.''

"You bet.''

"You think we'll see a cougar?''

Please, God, no. "Could be.'' Nate was still look- ing at him expectantly, so Blake tried to inject more enthusiasm. "Yeah, could be,'' he repeated.

"Uncle John said there were wolves back in these parts.''

"So I've heard. I always thought wolves got an unfair reputation for being trouble. Personally I tend to think they're good critters.''

"Me, too. I think they're good. I guess I think just like you, huh, Dr. Blake?'' Like a real trooper, Nate gathered up the tent stakes.

"You know how to do this, huh?'' Blake tried to sound like a supportive adult instead of so pitifully hopeful.

"Well, sure. Nothing to putting up a tent for us frontier guys, right? But then we gotta get our fire started. You know how it is. You can't cook for for- ever, because at first the fire's so big and everything'd burn. So you gotta get it started.''

"You sound like a real pro.''

"Yeah, I am. But you camped a lot, too, didn't you?''

"When I was your age, yes,'' Blake admitted. "I

used to love it. Sleeping under the stars. Cooking out-side. Hiking places where no one had been.''

"Yeah, me, too. Just like that."

''But I just haven't had a chance to do it in a while. Once I started medical school…well, there just wasn't time. And for a lot of years I was living in the city.''

"Oh. That's too bad." Nate looked at him pen-sively, obviously trying to figure out something con-soling to say. "I have a friend named George. He had to live in the city for a while, too."

"Oh, yeah?"

"He came back to the mountains last year. He's okay now, but it took a while. I think it— Hey, what's wrong?"

''I—''

Shock blocked his throat. He felt the sting, which in itself was nothing, but it was as if lightning zapped the back of his calf and sent a jolt of electricity all through his body in a millisecond. That fast, his vi-sion blurred and his heart pounded. That fast, he could barely see the bee that had stung him.

"Uh-oh, uh-oh. Dr. Blake, what's wrong? Some-thing's wrong!"

"Don't be scared. A bee just stung me." He sank to the ground, feeling his blood rush like a boiling river. In principle, even if he hadn't been a doctor, he would have known precisely what to do. Get the stinger out, pronto, then lift his calf higher than his heart. He had to do the first-aid things, and fast. Panic clutched his pulse that he could desert his son—a six-year-old little boy—if he passed out, and he just couldn't keep any other thoughts in his head. He forced his voice to sound calm. ''Nate?''

''You're sick? You get sick like me if a bee stings you?''

''Yes. I have exactly the same allergy to bees that you do. I carry a shot with me…but it's in my backpack, Nate. Could you get it for me? Right now, really quick, okay?''

''Okay, okay! I got my shot, too! I brung it, 'cause my mom says I always have to bring the shot on camping trips now. And I know how to use it. I know everything. Don't you worry, Dr. Blake. I'm here! I'll save you!''

The sky started dancing. Blake felt his whole body coat with a layer of clammy, sticky sweat. His head couldn't seem to hold itself up, and his calf seemed assaulted by nonstop bolts of fire.

He had to stay conscious. He wasn't going to fail Nate, not again. This time he had to prove himself to his son; there may never be another chance. Passing out wasn't an option. There was no way in hell he was leaving a six-year-old boy alone at dusk in the middle of nowhere, scared to death, and with an unconscious man to worry about, besides.

''See, Dr. Blake? See?'' Small, sturdy legs hunched down next to him. A hypodermic waved in front of his eyes. ''That's my shot, see? First you squeeze to get out the air, until you can see the medicine come out, right? And then you got stung in the leg, so I have to give you the shot in the leg, right? Up above where you got stung. O'course, it's gonna hurt. All shots hurt. But it's okay if you cry. Nobody's here but me. Okay?''

Okayokayokay. Dizzy, he lifted a hand to touch his son's face. There seemed to be nothing in his mind but that silly litany of okay's. *Stay conscious, stay conscious. Don't fail Serena. Not again.* And those soft, blue eyes, just like his own, kept looking at him. His son. His beautiful son. But when he opened this mouth to answer Nate's questions, nothing came out.

Everything went black.

Serena slammed out of her truck, jet-streamed past the landmark statue of Lewis and Clark, and barreled through the doors of the Whitehorn Memorial Hospital.

If there was a time in the week the hospital would be crowded, it was Saturday night. Still running, she saw a frantic mom pacing in a waiting room, a small boy with a black eye holding a dog, Collin Kincaid helping in a hurt ranch hand. She saw. But she said hello to no one, her throat too thick and her pulse too frantic to try talking, even to folks she'd known all her life.

The volunteer at the front desk could see she was upset, even if her shower-damp hair and yanked-on

T-shirt weren't an obvious indication. "The sheriff called me. I'm Serena Dovesong. My son—Nate Dovesong—and Blake Remmington. They came in together, but I don't know—"

"Yes, dear. I believe someone on the second floor had your son for a bit. The little one was hungry, and Dr. Remmington needed to be examined. But by now they should be in the same room—"

"Which is…"

"Two-oh-four, dear. Try to relax. Your son's fine. In fact, both of them are going to be fine. It's after visiting hours, so it's quiet upstairs…"

The woman was still talking, but Serena stopped hearing after registering the room number. She whisked past the elevator and tore up the stairs. Her pulse was pounding louder than a carpenter's hammer in her ears, anxiety slamming in her chest. She told herself it was stupid to worry. The sheriff had told her that Nate was perfectly okay, that Blake had been stung by a bee and had to stay overnight but that he would be all right, too. She got it. Nobody was dying. Nothing that terrible had happened. But no matter how many times she repeated those reassurances to herself, she wanted her eyes on Nate and Blake, and she wanted that now.

The instant she pushed open the stairwell door, she saw the nurses' station and immediately started tracking the room numbers…and then there it was—204.

Inside, there were two beds. No shades had been

drawn on the cloudless black night, and city lights winked outside. Blake was lying, too still, on one bed, his eyes closed, his leg elevated under the stark white sheet. She surged toward him, a knife of fear instinctively stabbing her heart. But he wasn't alone in the room.

Although her eyes had a hard time cutting away from Blake, her son was in the first bed. He lay back, watching a cop show with a dish of ice cream in one hand and some kind of fizzy pop in the other. Before either could even say hi, she had her arms wrapped around Nate tighter than a stranglehold.

"Hey, Mom!" Nate survived the hug and the kiss. He even lit up when he first saw her, but then his face fell. "You aren't gonna make me go home, are you? I'm having a great time."

"So the sheriff was telling me." She tried to breathe normally again. Once absolutely positive her son was okay, she leaned back against Blake's bed, touched his wrist, his hand. They had an IV going into his arm, and his skin looked pale, but he seemed to be breathing and sleeping normally. Enough for her to smile for her son. "From what I heard, you're a hero. I can't wait for you to tell me all about it."

"Well, it was so cool, Mom. I got to give him a shot and everything, just like I was the doctor. And he just went plonk, crashed on the ground. It was because of a bee."

"So the sheriff said. And from what I understood, you saved his life."

"Well, yeah. He's my dad, after all."

Serena's lips had been parted to ask for more story details, but now her mouth clamped shut. She tried to swallow. "What'd you just say?"

"I said, yeah, he's my dad. You know. That's what made it important to be brave. I got to ride next to the sheriff. With the siren on. Just me and him, 'cause they put Dr. Blake in the ambulance. That wasn't scary, it was fun. I started to cry when they told me I couldn't go with him, but once we got to the hospital, after a while they let me be in here with him. He just has to sleep, so I got a job. It's my job to make sure nothing bothers him. They put tons and tons of med'cine into him and he just keeps snoozing."

Serena was still struggling to swallow. "Sweetheart, a second ago you called Dr. Blake your dad."

"Yeah, well." He peered into his ice cream dish as if annoyed it was empty, then set it on the bed tray and flopped back. For a young man up way past his bedtime, he looked as happy as a self-indulgent sultan. An extremely dirty sultan. "I figured you guys were gonna tell me about it sooner or later. I just thought maybe I wasn't supposed to talk about it until you said."

It was a good thing Serena was leaning on the bed. "But, honey, how did you know that Dr. Blake—"

"Was my dad? Because of everything. We get sick the same way when we're stung by bees. And especially in the beginning, he was so goofy around me. Just sitting and looking at me sometimes for no reason. And listening to every single thing I said. I mean, there had to be a reason he was that weird. I'm a kid. Nobody listens to kids. Not normal people, anyway. And then you guys were so yucky together."

"Yucky?"

"Come on, Mom. Gimme a break. He always looked at you all mushy. It just kept getting worse. It was enough to make a guy gag. Anyway, even a dumb kid could have figured it all out ages ago."

"And you're smart."

"Yeah, I'm smart." Nate never doubted that his mom appreciated this. "And I haven't had a chance to tell you the scary part yet. Not that I was scared. But when he went plonk? I didn't know what to do, because I couldn't wake him up and he couldn't talk to me and it was starting to get dark—"

"Sweetheart, what did you do?"

Nate grinned with macho satisfaction. "I remembered that he was a doctor. And he had to have a phone, right? Because docs have phones. And I knew where his car was. Although that was the scary part, because it was a ways to the car and it was getting dark and there were bears and all...but then all I had to do was dial 9-1-1 and 'splain to the lady."

"I'm so proud of you for being so brave. And for

doing the right thing when you were scared.'' Poor baby. He had to suffer through another strangling love hug from his mom. "You know what, Nate? That's just what your dad would have done.''

"Yeah. He's probably gonna be so proud of me that he can't stand it,'' Nate announced with a world-weary sigh. "I'll probably have to tell him the story over and over about how brave I was and everything.''

"I think you're right. In fact, I know you are. But in the meantime, how do you feel about him being your dad?''

"Sheesh, Mom. You know. I've been waiting for my dad to come find me my whole life. I was just scared he wouldn't like me, you know? And then I couldn't figure out why you guys didn't tell me so I could call him Dad. And I started to worry maybe he didn't want me to call him Dad.''

"Oh, Nate!''

"It's okay. I quit thinking about it. I mean, he thinks I'm great, you know? He tells me and tells me. And he's way happy to be with me, you can see. So I just figured you grown-ups would have to figure out the rest, the way grown-ups do. One thing, though, Mom.''

"What, hon?''

"I think he wants to live with us. But I think he's too shy to ask you. And I was thinking…''

"You've been doing a lot of thinking," Serena murmured.

"Uh-huh. I was thinking that I could put the computer in my bedroom. Then Dr. Blake could have the den for his own bedroom. So we already have enough space for him, you know?"

Her son seemed to have a dozen plans for his dad. And it suddenly occurred to Serena that she had just as many plans for Blake, but so far, she hadn't found the courage to say them out loud. Not to the one who mattered. In fact, not to either of the males she loved more than life.

But that was about to change.

Fast.

For a woman who'd always embraced risk with both hands open, Serena suddenly understood why Blake had been hung up for so long on doing the right thing. It wasn't so easy to move when your heart was perched precariously over a cliff with no safety net below.

But she loved that man. And no matter how Serena considered the immediate decisions confronting her, that love provided the only answer she had—and the only choice.

Blake could have sworn it was still midnight, but he opened his eyes to a stunning wall of sunshine. It took several moments to catalog his surroundings and get his bearings. The last thing he remembered was being on Kincaid land with Nate, the dark falling fast, the bee sting, praying he'd stay conscious for his son's sake.

His mind was still fuzzy with drugs, but it didn't take a doctor to recognize a hospital room. His leg was still swollen some, but the bee sting site no longer felt like a concentrated forest fire. He was just raising a hand to push off the sheet when he saw her. Serena. Curled up in a chair, a pillow wedged against the wall, her bare toes in sight under an ivory sweater that she was using for a blanket.

She made his heart stop, she was so beautiful. The sunlight pouring in made her hair shine like black gold, brushed her cheek, dipped some of that light into the open collar of her shirt. The pale blue shirt was wrinkled, her eyes had soft smudges from tiredness, and her mouth was so soft, so perfect, that he just wanted to stare at her and never stop.

Then thoughts started bulleting through his mind. Serena had clearly been here for hours. She was here for him, when the only thing he ever wanted to do for Serena was be there, the same way. Instead he'd failed her yet again and jeopardized her son. Their son. Their six-year-old was the hero, not the man who'd wanted to be her hero so badly.

Until that moment his mind had never put the hero thing into words, but for him it was like a birthmark. His whole life, it had been part of him. He'd never had family to cling to, never had role models in the men in his life, yet he had always understood that if you did the right thing, you could stand tall. Of all the people on the planet he'd wanted to stand tall for, though, there was only one who really mattered to him. Her. The one who made him feel wicked. The one who opened up his life to all the wicked, wonderful possibilities. The one person who had always made him feel good about himself, no matter who he really was or wasn't.

It wouldn't bother him to fail someone else. Some failures happened in life; Blake was too old to fret being human. But not her. The only one he never wanted to fail was her, and he had from the beginning, getting her pregnant and then failing to be part of the picture. And now, last night, he'd risked their son.

Her eyes suddenly fluttered open, squinted against the vibrantly stunning sunlight and then found him across the room. Immediately she pushed out of the chair, her sweater dropping to the floor as she hustled toward him. "Well, Doc. I'll be darned. You almost look human this morning."

"I almost feel human this morning." Human enough to ache just from the touch of her hand. "Where's our boy?"

She leaned a hip on the bed, her fingers still threaded with his. "Nate's with his uncle Wolf, but I'll tell you, he left here under major protest. He didn't want to leave you at all. He also didn't want to leave the nurses, who were giving him ice cream and cookies and pop on demand.'' Her fingers squeezed his. ''You'd better be prepared before seeing him this afternoon.''

His heart braced. ''Prepared for what?''

''He's going to want to tell you the story about saving your life at least five thousand times. And then another five thousand. We're going to be creaking in our rocking chairs before he gets tired of telling it. And then there's another little thing you'd better be prepared for.''

''What?''

''He knows,'' she said softly. ''He figured it out weeks ago—that you were his dad. And he likes it.''

''He couldn't like it.''

''Oh, yeah, he does, Blake. In fact, the way he put it to me…he's been waiting for you to find him his whole life.''

He squeezed his eyes closed, well aware that his mind was still foggy around the edges. ''Serena, don't mess with me right now. I can't think that clearly.''

But he could feel. The weight of her thigh on the bed. The texture of her slim, warm fingers tenting with his. The scent of her drifting on the morning sunlight, a little sandalwood, a little jasmine, a little pure Serena. Desire stirred in him, when it couldn't. The antihistamine was still spinning his mind and his leg hurt like a cussword and he felt as though his worst fear had come true as far as being a failure...a failure in her eyes.

No part of him could possibly have been aroused.

Yet he was.

And when she tightened her hand, he was more aroused yet.

"You think I'm lying to you?" she murmured.

"I think I haven't done one right thing by Nate. Or you. No matter how hard I tried. But I'm sorry, Serena. So sorry that—"

"Sorry that you forced that bee to sting you?"

He frowned in confusion. "No, of course not. But that Nate was left alone and in such a dangerous position—"

"Ah. Then it *was* your fault the bee stung you."

He let out an exasperated sigh. "Don't make fun."

For a few seconds she regarded him in silence, studying his face, his eyes. And then she said calmly, deliberately, "The nurse popped in about an hour ago. She checked your blood pressure and so on. I imagine you must feel like you were hit with a steamroller, from how they described your allergic reaction to me. But she said you're doing great."

"Then I'm getting out of here." He tried pushing at the sheet again, at least until she shook a finger at him.

"Nope. Not until you're released by the doctor, and he won't be in to check you out until sometime after ten this morning."

"I *am* a doctor. And I'm fine. I just need a minute to get my head together."

"The nurse said you'd try to cause trouble." Blake felt bereft when she moved her hand away and stood up. "She said you were a horrible patient last night. That everyone knows doctors make the worse patients, but you were really bad." He watched her walk over to the door and deliberately push it closed. "You're staying until you're released by the doc, and that's that."

He tried another fake scowl on her. "Did I know you had this bossy streak before?"

"You ain't seen nothing yet, love."

Love. The word suddenly shimmered in the air between them like a perfumed gauntlet. Particularly when she came back, still barefoot, and perched on the hospital bed again, even closer than before.

"Something's happening here," he mentioned.

"Yeah, there is. I realize that you're not feeling at all well yet...but sometimes a problem just won't wait for a convenient time. It needs to be handled immediately. Do you know what your son told me?"

"No, what?"

"That he wants to move the computer into his bedroom, so that we can free up the den for you. So you can come live with us and have your own room."

"Uh-oh."

"That was exactly my reaction. Uh-oh. Nate also said that he thought you were too shy to ask about coming to live with us, so I needed to do it. He didn't coach me, but I think he had something like this in mind.'' He felt the graze of her fingertips on his whiskery cheek, the stroke of a kiss in the way she looked at him. ''Would you come be with us…be the husband of my heart and the father of my son and the hero that I happen to desperately love?''

He suddenly forgot how to breathe. ''Serena, I think I'm light-headed.''

''Now don't start getting worried. I wouldn't really ask you that. I've told you before I could never be with a man if he felt beholden. Like he *had* to be with me. Like he owed me. So that's out of the question, but the problem, Blake, is that your son thinks you need to be living with us.''

''Damn. I must be having some kind of medication reaction, because now I seem to be imagining things. Hallucinating. Hearing voices.''

''Yeah, and you're gonna hear a lot more voices before this is over, Doc.'' She leaned over him. So close that he could see the emotion blazing in her eyes. See her disheveled hair sweeping like a black satin cape over her shoulder. See her lips coming toward him. The kiss was softer than silver. ''You don't have to do anything to be loved, Blake.''

''Pardon?''

''I always understood why you felt you had to prove yourself. You had two fathers who didn't know how to love. But that was their flaw, not yours. Their loss, not yours. You never had to prove anything. You were always worth loving.''

He wiped a hand over his face. ''Is this lecture in lieu of anything?''

''Yes. It's a warning and a threat. Which isn't a fair thing to do to a man who was as sick as you were last night, but that's how the cookie crumbles.''

If she was going to look at him that way, she could threaten him from now until eternity and he'd ask for more. ''Okay. So what is this particular threat?''

Her smile disappeared. ''You either say the right words to me, Blake, or I'm out that door. For good. And that really isn't a threat. It's a promise.''

She could, he thought, have some mercy on a man as sick as he'd been. Yet he saw no mercy in her eyes. Her expression was dominated by an emotion. A singular, consuming emotion. He couldn't doubt how seriously she meant this test. ''Serena?''

''What?''

His tongue felt thick, his throat rusty. ''I love you. I love you more than my life. When you're in the same room, my soul feels bigger, my life, all the possibilities. When you leave the room, all the shadows come back. I'm not the man I want to be. The joy in life is never the same, because you are the joy of my life and you have been from the day I met you.''

Tears misted her eyes. ''Damn it, Blake, if you felt like that, why couldn't you have said one word about it long before this?''

"Because you had that issue thing. About feeling beholden. And because...because you're everything. I couldn't imagine how you could need me. You're sunshine on the inside. You love everything about life. You're not afraid of anything. What could I ever have to offer you?"

"The only thing I ever wanted," she whispered.

"A hundred million men could love you, and all of them'd be better than me."

"See? That's where you're all screwed up. And I warned you. I'm leaving—out that door for good—unless you say the right words instead of the wrong ones."

"All right, all right." Sweat—possibly from the allergic reaction—dotted his forehead. He hooked a gentle fist around the rope of her hair, not pulling, not even grasping hard. Just willing her not to leave. It was a second before he could breathe past the panic that she could walk away from him. "Would you marry me?"

"Humph. I can't imagine why. Everybody gets married these days, then divorced a few years later. It's too much trouble, and for what? I make a living. I can support our son. And I can certainly love someone without a piece of paper in my hand."

There was a sudden knock on the door. "Dr. Remmington? This is Nurse Hathway."

"Go away."

"We're supposed to bring your breakfast in."

"I don't want breakfast and I don't want anyone in here." He never stopped looking at Serena. "I need an hour alone."

The nurse obviously wasn't budging that easily. "Serena? Are you in there?"

"Yes."

"Oh. Okay, then."

Again there was silence, then the thud of quiet footprints. And then nothing, but his eyes facing her eyes. "I don't give a damn about a piece of paper, either. It's not a nice, safe, legal marriage I want with you. I'm asking you a different kind of question entirely."

"So? Spill out what you mean."

"I'm asking you to create a marriage with me of nonstop, gigantic risks. I want someone to climb mountains with. Someone to not feel safe with. Someone with whom I can explore all the emotions there are, all the possibilities. Someone with whom I can even risk fighting with."

"Even that?"

For the gentle teasing in her voice, he had to kiss her. He was feeling better than he first thought. In fact, he was feeling superb. Coaxing her down beside him wasn't even a challenge, and her lips melded against his as if they'd always been a matched pair. He tasted promise in her kiss. He tasted their future. He tasted love, as he'd never dreamed love could ever happen in his life.

"You're my heart, Serena. The only person where

I ever felt like I belonged. If I could love you every day of my life, it'd still never be enough. I want to give you sons and daughters. I want to make volcanoes in your kitchen, and make love in your yard when the kids are finally asleep. I want to make you feel wicked, the way you've always make me feel wicked.''

''Wicked?''

Momentarily she looked confused. Serenely happy and content, but confused. Clearly he needed to illustrate exactly what she'd always done to him. If she didn't quite get it this time, Blake figured they had a lifetime to get those kinds of minor details straight.

Now he had a woman to cherish, and he wanted to be absolutely sure that he did it right.

# Epilogue

Cold was spitting in the air. Just a taste. The wind had a bite, the stiff breeze was fresh and invigorating. Not that Nate needed anything to energize him. He'd been running circles around Blake since they'd left the car.

"We can be here a whole other hour, right, Dad?"

Blake still wasn't used to hearing that "dad" word. It still clutched him in the chest every time. "A good hour, I promise," he affirmed.

Nate had come to love this private stretch of Kincaid land, as Blake had once hoped. Weeks ago Nate had informed him that it was "sacred land" because it was where he'd saved Blake's life. And they needed to go back "a lot" to pick up the "good vibes."

"And by then Mom'll be back from the doc, right?"

"Yup. She should be." Blake watched as Nate swooped up the hillside, arms outstretched, and then made like an airplane and flew back down.

"What I don't get is how come she's going to a doctor. When you're a doctor. And I don't get why we should have to ever go to any other doctor when you're right here in our family.''

"Well, this is a different kind of doctor, Nate. I like to work especially with kids, like we talked about before. So that makes me a pediatrician. But the kind of doctor your mom is visiting today has a speciality for grown-up women.''

"So why's she going?''

"There's nothing to worry about, son. She's just getting a check-up.''

"Uh-huh.'' Nate stopped whooping it up and down knolls long enough to heave a world-weary sigh. "I don't know why you guys don't tell me things, when I'm very very smart and I already know. She's throwing up a lot. That's why she's going to the doc, right?''

"You're right. You're very smart. And I'm sorry we hid that from you. I should have realized you'd figure it out.''

"I know. I figure everything out.'' Nate threw himself on a grassy spot, finally tuckered out for at least a minute.

Blake sank down next to him, his big hiking boots nudging his son's. They'd gotten the same brand. "This throwing up thing doesn't mean she's sick or that there's anything to worry about.''

"I know, I know. She's laughing and giggling all the time. I'd know if my mom were sick.'' Nate turned his head and squinted. "You'd know if my mom were sick, too. You can tell when you love somebody. Did you know that?''

"I'm beginning to learn a lot of things from you, Nate,'' Blake said quietly.

"Well, sure. We teach each other. And hey, Dad, by the way, do we have to go to Cade and Leanne's wedding on Saturday?''

"Yup, we do.''

"But do we have to get dressed up?''

"Afraid so, son.''

"Yech. We could call and say we're sick. And then we could come here and camp out. Not Mom. She likes all these weddings. But you and me still could.''

"Well, I can't say I'm real fond of getting dressed up myself. But remember the last wedding? How much fun you had? Don't you like your grandpa Garrett? And all your new cousins?''

"Well, yeah. They're fun. And I like Gramps a lot. I had the best time at our wedding that I ever had in my whole life. Except for the night I saved you and all. Nothin'll ever be as good as that and— Oh!'' Nate's hand fumbled in his jacket pocket, and emerged with a wadded-up, crumpled piece of paper. "I keep forgetting to give you this. It's for you. It's from school.''

Dutifully, Blake took the paper, turning to shield it from the wind. He wasn't sure that paper was going to survive trying to unfold it, but judging from the last artwork Nate had brought home, it was likely to be nip-and-tuck guessing what the picture was no matter what shape the masterpiece was in.

Right then, Nate hadn't stopped talking anyway. "I'll bet you didn't r'lize that I could read and write, did you? But I've been in school for weeks now, so I know how. I just didn't have a chance to tell you yet, because there's always so much I want to tell you. Anyway, we had to write a story. So this is my first story ever in my whole life. Mom said I should give it to you."

For the first time in two months—possibly longer—Nate fell silent. He looked at Blake, then away. Then at Blake again. Nate scratched his cheek, then sighed, then itched his knee, then looked at Blake again.

Blake managed to unfold the sheet of paper. Instead of artwork, there was printing on this particular school project. At the top of the page, in gigantic letters, it said, "My Hero." The *M* in "my" had an extra scoop, and the *H* took up half of the entire line. Below that was a single sentence. "My dad is my hero."

And that was it.

The whole story.

Except for Nate's name printed in the upper right-hand corner. With only two erasures.

Nate scuffed some dirt, then itched his cheek again, then blurted, "Sheesh. Whatsa matter? You're not sick, are you?"

"No. I'm not sick." It was just hard for a heart to

swell this big without bursting. And the lump in his throat was as big as a slug. His life had never been that terrible, but he'd never dreamed what a life could really be until he'd known Serena's love. Serena, Nate, their building and exploring all the relationships in the Kincaid family…Blake felt as if his world was exploding every day, getting bigger, brighter, limitless in the possibilities.

Always, though, he had a hard time shaking his Achilles' heel. His love for Nate was as fierce as a warrior's. He'd have done anything for his son. But what he wanted to do, more than anything, was to be a good father for Nate. The kind of father he'd never had himself. The kind of father he wasn't positive that he knew how to be, no matter how many times Serena reassured him. Yeah, he knew Nate got on with him. But seeing those words in that precious first-grade handwriting damn near took him out.

"Dad—"

"I'm not sick," he repeated. "I just couldn't talk for a second. You really touched me, Nate. I'm honored that you wrote this story."

"Well, actually we had to write the story," Nate said with his brand of relentless honesty. "But what we got to choose was who was our hero. Some kids really had to think, but not me. I knew right away it had to be you. You know what makes a hero?"

"No. Tell me."

"A dad who wants to be with his kid. That's what a hero is. Where you don't have to be afraid of the dark, because you know your dad'll come. And if you're dirty and you know your mom's gonna be mad, you can tell your dad 'cause he'll try and fix it for you. A dad'll even try to make her laugh so she'll forget about being mad. And a dad wants to hear when you have important things to say. And you know what most of all?''

"What, Nate?"

"He loves you. And you know that every day, so you don't have to worry about it. It's just there. You never have to worry about it as long as you live. Do you think it's time to pick up Mom, yet? Because I think I'm getting hungry.''

"Me, too.'' Blake lurched to his feet and then held out his hands. Nate's grin nearly split his face wide. He knew the ritual. The two males did a fancy high-five—their own private secret handshake—and then Blake swung his son onto his shoulders and started hiking downhill. Toward home.

Toward Serena.

And, just maybe, toward the chance of a new brother or sister for Nate.

*MONTANA MAVERICKS:*
*WED IN WHITEHORN*

continues next month with

**THE MARRIAGE BARGAIN**
*by Victoria Pade*

*Turn the page for
an exciting preview...*

# One

Victoria Rutherford had fantasized about her wedding day since she was a little girl. She'd imagined that she'd wear a beautiful white off-the-shoulder gown with a wide, lacy skirt and a ten-foot train trailing behind her. She'd pictured her father walking her proudly down the aisle of a candlelit cathedral decorated with flowers and filled to the brim with friends and family. She'd dreamed of a groom waiting at the end of that aisle who watched her approach with a beaming smile on his handsome face, a groom who loved her so much she could feel it emanating from him.

Well, that might have been what she'd fantasized about, imagined, pictured and dreamed of, but it definitely wasn't how this wedding would be.

Her wedding.

That wasn't how her wedding would be in any way, shape or form.

Because there she was, standing in a public rest room across the hall from the judge's chambers where the ceremony would begin in ten minutes. And rather than a beautiful white off-the-shoulder gown, she was wearing just what she'd been dressed in when she'd arrived in her old hometown of Whitehorn, Montana, early that morning—navy-blue slacks and a light-weight pale blue sweater set.

There would be no gown. No cathedral full of well-wishers. No proud father to give her away.

And there certainly wouldn't be a beaming groom emoting a great love for her.

Never in her wildest fantasies, imaginings, picturings, or dreams had it occurred to her that part of the real estate deal she'd come to Whitehorn to take care of on behalf of her mother and terribly ill father would have involved getting married this afternoon.

The shock of it all showed on her face as she stared at herself in the rest room mirror. Her normally healthy peaches-and-cream skin was pale. Her usually lush lips were washed-out, too. Only her blue eyes and what she considered reasonably long eyelashes offered any color at all. Even her wavy blond hair seemed to have lost its life, falling to just below her shoulders much more limply than it had when she'd left her father's bedside in Denver at dawn.

"Some bride you'll make," she said to her reflection.

Then again, under the circumstances, what could she expect?

Who forced a person to marry him these days? she asked herself, still reeling from what had transpired since her arrival in Whitehorn.

She'd come back to the Montana town to do what

ill health prevented her parents from doing—sign the papers that sold their once profitable but now failing ranch.

In its glory days the ranch had been home to her, her mother Clarissa and her father Charles. A glorious home that had provided an income substantial enough to launch her father into several other business ventures and make him a wealthy man. One of the wealthiest in Whitehorn.

But then her dad had gotten sick with degenerative kidney disease and his medical expenses had begun to drain away everything.

Her father had always been in robust health and hadn't seen a reason to carry more than the bare minimum of medical insurance. He'd been sure that he would always be able to afford whatever the insurance didn't cover should he or his wife become ill.

But he'd underestimated just how expensive prolonged medical care could be.

In the three years since he'd gotten sick he'd had to sell off everything but the ranch to foot the bills. He'd held on to it even though he and Victoria's mother had had to move to Denver to be near the dialysis treatments that were keeping him alive.

But the ranch had been generating far fewer profits without her father running it, and had, in fact, become a strain on her parents' already overburdened financial situation.

Victoria had helped out where she could, but a college philosophy teacher's salary, even at Boston University, was hardly enough to pick up the slack. And so, reluctantly, her parents had opted to sell the ranch.

Although Victoria hadn't been in on the decision, she didn't doubt that it had been a sad day when it was made. She knew how much her father had loved that ranch. She knew that nothing short of desperate need would have brought him to that point, despite his denial that the need was all that desperate.

So the ranch had gone up for sale.

Within two weeks a buyer had made an offer. By proxy. None of them had realized how important the cloak of that proxy was.

Until today when Victoria had learned the truth.

Well, part of it, anyway.

She'd learned who was lurking behind that proxy and what were his terms for finalizing the sale, though not why he was setting those terms.

Adam Benson was the buyer.

"Adam Benson," she whispered to the mirror, as if she'd have more luck getting it to sink in if she said his name out loud.

There are people in every life who aren't forgotten. Who can't be forgotten, no matter how hard you try. For Victoria, Adam Benson was one of those.

Victoria remembered Adam Benson, the son of a man her father had hired as a ranch hand and her mother's maid long ago. She remembered him and what she'd done to him, to his whole family.

She never thought of him without feeling ashamed of herself. And guilty. Very, very guilty.

She would have thought she was the last person on earth whom he would want anything to do with. And for good reason. But instead, he was making the sale of the ranch contingent upon one thing—her marrying him.

"It's crazy," she told her image in the mirror. Totally and completely crazy.

Maybe the man had gone insane since the last time she'd seen him when they were both teenagers.

But he hadn't seemed insane when she'd met with him that morning at his insistence. Cold. Calculating. Arrogant. But not insane.

She hadn't found it strange when the Realtor had said the buyer wanted a moment alone with her before signing the papers. She'd figured he might want to ask when the furniture would be removed or who among the ranch hands was worth keeping and who wasn't. Something simple, innocent.

In her wildest dreams it had never occurred to her that she would find herself alone in a room with Adam Benson.

The years had been kind to him—that was the first thing that had struck her when she'd recognized him. He'd always been a good-looking guy and time had only improved upon that.

He was tall—Victoria judged him to be at least six-two—and had a muscular, athletic body in a suit that had to have cost four thousand dollars if it cost a penny. His shoulders were broad and straight, blocking her view of anything behind him. His waist was narrow, his hips lean, and his legs long and thick.

He was solid, substantial, imposing, commanding. He'd become a man who filled a room all by himself. Whose power infused it and left no doubt that he was calling the shots and would have it no other way.

Maturity had chiseled his features to sharply honed lines. His cheekbones were high and his entire jawbone was so defined and strong that she thought one tilt of his prominent chin was enough to make other men pause.

His lower lip was slightly fuller than his upper, but, oh, what a divinely sensuous curve that upper one had developed just below a nose that was finer than any surgeon could ever sculpt.

His hair was raven-black and he wore it short on the sides, barely long enough on top to comb back and all so impeccable she'd wondered if he had it cut every day.

As if all that wasn't enough, dark brows arched over penetrating gray eyes the color of pewter. Eyes that hadn't left her from the moment she'd walked into the room. Eyes that hadn't wavered. Or warmed.

He'd laid out his terms then, in what Victoria had learned right away was actually a business meeting. A business meeting in which he had the upper hand. A business meeting that began and ended with an ultimatum—marry him and the deal went through.

Reject him and it didn't.

If she rejected him, not only did she nix the deal

with him, but he assured her that he would use his wealth, power and influence to block the sale of the ranch to anyone else.

At first Victoria had thought he was out of his mind and hadn't taken either his ultimatum or his threat seriously. How could he prevent the sale to anyone else? He had no hold over her or her family or the ranch.

"One phone call," he'd assured her mildly, confidently. "Do you think any bank anywhere in the world would turn down a deposit of a couple million from me if all I'm asking in return is that they deny a loan to any buyer of yours?"

Cold. Calculating. Arrogant.

And deadly serious.

Victoria didn't know what had happened to Adam Benson in the years since he and his family had left Whitehorn. But she did know he had cash for the million-and-a-half offer he'd made for the ranch. And from the looks of him, that million and a half was pocket change.

She didn't doubt he had the money to make good on his threat.

But marry him? Why would he want her to marry him?

She'd asked that point blank.

But he hadn't given her an answer. Instead, one side of that sensuous mouth had raised in a slow smile that was more smug and satisfied than amused.

All he'd said was, "Those are my terms. Marry

me, we sign the marriage certificate first, then the papers for the sale. Or no deal.''

It just didn't make any sense.

She hadn't believed what she was hearing.

And yet there he'd been, standing right in front of her, dwarfing her five-foot-six-inch frame and laying out his ultimatum as if he were demanding nothing more than the inclusion of the refrigerator in the sale.

She'd never envisioned herself as a home appliance and so had not jumped to agree to what he was insisting.

Her hesitation had inspired the playing of more of his hand.

He'd pulled out her parents' financial statements—something she had no idea how he'd gotten hold of, something she'd never seen herself. They proved in black and white just how much her parents needed the deal to go through, more even than they'd let her know.

As if that wasn't enough, he'd upped the ante with projections of the future costs of keeping her father alive.

In short, Adam Benson had let her know that he had her just where he wanted her and wasn't above coming in for the kill.

And this was the man she was going to marry.

That thought sent a chill through her veins.

Because no matter how good-looking he was—and he *was* drop-dead gorgeous—he was alarmingly austere. The slight air of the bad boy that had been so alluring when they were teenagers had taken on a much harder edge. Now he seemed downright dangerous.

He *was* dangerous, she reminded herself. He was dangerous to her family's future.

Which meant one thing in Victoria's mind—she didn't have any choice but to marry Adam Benson. Whether she understood why he was pushing for it or not, whether she liked it or not.

"So buck up, because this is what you have to do," she told her reflection, noticing that her thoughts about this whole thing had washed even more color out of her face.

A knock on the rest room door made her jump and realize once more how unnerved she was by what she was about to do.

"Miss Rutherford?" came a voice from outside the door, a man's voice that she recognized as that of Adam Benson's assistant. "Mr. Benson says it's time for the ceremony."

Victoria's heart felt as if it were in her throat.

*Time for the ceremony...*

He might as well have said "The gallows are ready for your hanging."

In her mind that was what this really seemed like. And she wasn't sure she could go through with it.

But then she thought about her parents, childhood sweethearts who still adored each other.

She thought about her dad, his indomitable spirit

and positive outlook still shining through even debilitating illness.

She thought of that financial statement Adam had produced that proved just how much they needed the money.

And she thought about the fact that she alone could make it happen. That she alone could ensure that her parents had what they needed.

She took a deep breath and held it until her face turned red and her shoulders had floated up as if attached to balloons. Then she exhaled and made sure her shoulders stayed there—straight and strong and determined—a miniature version of Adam Benson's own shoulders.

"I can do this," she told herself. No matter why he wanted her to. "I can do this."

The assistant knocked and called her name again.

Victoria pushed herself away from the counter where her hands had been clutching the edge without her even realizing it. She marched to the door, opened it and held her chin high as she crossed the hall to the judge's chambers where Adam Benson waited for her.

Lethally handsome.

Cold as stone.

Somehow when she looked up at his face and took her place by his side, she couldn't help thinking that this was only the beginning of what he had planned for her....

USA Today Bestselling Author

# SHARON SALA

has won readers' hearts with thrilling tales
of romantic suspense. Now Silhouette Books
is proud to present five passionate stories from
this beloved author.

Available in August 2000:
### ALWAYS A LADY
A beauty queen whose dreams have been dashed in a
tragic twist of fate seeks shelter for her wounded spirit
in the arms of a rough-edged cowboy....

Available in September 2000:
### GENTLE PERSUASION
A brooding detective risks everything to protect the
woman he once let walk away from him....

Available in October 2000:
### SARA'S ANGEL
A woman on the run searches desperately for a reclusive
Native American secret agent—the only man who can save
her from the danger that stalks her!

Available in November 2000:
### HONOR'S PROMISE
A struggling waitress discovers she is really a rich heiress—
and must enter a powerful new world of wealth and
privilege on the arm of a handsome stranger....

Available in December 2000:
### KING'S RANSOM
A lone woman returns home to the ranch where she was
raised, and discovers danger—as well as the man she once
loved with all her heart....

**Don't miss
an exciting opportunity
to save on the purchase of
Harlequin and Silhouette books!**

Buy any two Harlequin or
Silhouette books and save
**$10.00 off** future Harlequin
and Silhouette purchases

OR

buy any three
Harlequin or Silhouette books
and save **$20.00 off** future
Harlequin and Silhouette purchases.

*Watch for details
coming in October 2000!*

PHQ400

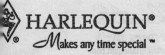

Coming Soon
Silhouette Books presents

*Weddings in White*

(on sale September 2000)

A 3-in-1 keepsake collection
by international bestselling author

# DIANA PALMER

Three heart-stoppingly handsome bachelors are paired
up with three innocent beauties who long to marry the
men of their dreams. This dazzling collection showcases
the enchanting characters and searing passion that
has made Diana Palmer a legendary talent
in the romance industry.

*Unlikely Lover:*

Can a feisty secretary and a gruff oilman fight
the true course of love?

*The Princess Bride:*

For better, for worse, starry-eyed Tiffany Blair captivated
Kingman Marshall's iron-clad heart....

*Callaghan's Bride:*

Callaghan Hart swore marriage was for fools—until
Tess Brady branded him with her sweetly seductive kisses!

*Available at your favorite retail outlet.*

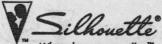

*Silhouette*®

*Where love comes alive*™

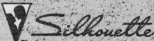

# MONTANA MAVERICKS

## WED IN WHITEHORN...
### where legends live on and love lasts forever!

If you missed either of the first two books in the
**MONTANA MAVERICKS** series, here's
a chance to order your copy today!

## MONTANA MAVERICKS

| | | |
|---|---|---|
| #65046 | **LONE STALLION'S LADY** by Lisa Jackson | $4.50 U.S.☐ $5.25 CAN.☐ |
| #65047 | **CHEYENNE BRIDE** by Laurie Paige | $4.50 U.S.☐ $5.25 CAN.☐ |

*(limited quantities available)*

| | |
|---|---|
| **TOTAL AMOUNT** | $ |
| **POSTAGE & HANDLING** | $ |
| ($1.00 for one book, 50¢ for each additional) | |
| **APPLICABLE TAXES\*** | $ _____ |
| **TOTAL PAYABLE** | $ _____ |
| (check or money order—please do not send cash) | |

To order, send the completed form, along with a check or money order for the total above,
payable to Montana Mavericks, to: **In the U.S.:** 3010 Walden Avenue, P.O. Box 9077, Buffalo,
NY 14269-9077 **In Canada:** P.O. Box 636, Fort Erie, Ontario L2A 5X3.

Name: _____

Address: _____ City: _____

State/Prov.: _____ Zip/Postal Code: _____

Account # (if applicable): _____ 075 CSAS

\*New York residents remit applicable sales taxes.
  Canadian residents remit applicable GST and provincial taxes.

### Silhouette®

Visit Silhouette at www.eHarlequin.com

MONMAVBACK2